Social Insecurity

By

James Shreve

PublishAmerica
Baltimore

© 2009 by James Shreve.
All rights reserved. No part of this book may be reproduced, stored in a retrieval system or transmitted in any form or by any means without the prior written permission of the publishers, except by a reviewer who may quote brief passages in a review to be printed in a newspaper, magazine or journal.

First printing

All characters in this book are fictitious, and any resemblance to real persons, living or dead, is coincidental.

PublishAmerica has allowed this work to remain exactly as the author intended, verbatim, without editorial input.

ISBN: 978-1-4489-2722-7 (softcover)
ISBN: 978-1-4489-9284-3 (hardcover)
PUBLISHED BY PUBLISHAMERICA, LLLP
www.publishamerica.com
Baltimore

Printed in the United States of America

This book is dedicated to the men and women of the USPS who deal with so much, some gracefully, some not.

Please don't look for any bungalows, motels or route numbers. I played fast and loose with the geography.

Acknowledgments

Thanks to the people in public relations for the Virginia State Police. You all were great! If there are any mistakes, they are mine.

Also, thanks to Alexandra Creamer, mi amiga, for checking the Spanish. Again, any mistakes are mine.

To my readers, Joy, Betsy and Bob, thank you. You are an extraordinary group. Also, Dawn, Jennifer and Steve, thank you for your friendship, kindness and all those little stickies on the pages that needed correcting.

Most of all, thank you to Toni, my wife, for her daily input, her secretarial skills, and being a sounding board for the ideas that helped me finish this book.

Prologue

Angel Iglesias pulled into the driveway, and drove into the dusty, brown overgrown farmyard. The grass had gone to seed and then died, and the weeds, the only things in the yard that would have been green, drooped under a cover of sand and dirt. It looked as if the grim reaper had decorated the place with thistle and roughstalk ryegrass.

He opened the cruiser door and, with one foot on the ground, grabbed his cowboy style hat and got out. Angel liked the light colored hat, which he donned as he walked the short path from the dirt to the house. Good guys wore hats like this.

A certain amount of trepidation accompanied him as he approached the house, something that accompanied him every day, in every new situation. Angel considered his apprehensiveness a friend, and he welcomed it as self-preservation, thinly disguised as fear. He enjoyed the adrenaline rush and the clarity of his senses.

Just be alert, he told himself. *You're going to be okay.*

His footsteps crunched the dirt, punctuating the clamorous buzz of insects that seemed unaware of the din they created. No dog barked, no chickens clucked. No goats, cats or cows animated the landscape. Angel mounted the uneven porch steps and tripped as a board beneath him sunk a half-inch. A black snake slithered rapidly out from under the steps and startled him. Catching himself, he felt his heart knocking like a broken rod in big V8. Angel took a moment to regain his composure. He knocked, and the weathered, wooden door of the old farmhouse swung in with a loud sound exaggerated by the stillness, like a croaking frog at a breeding pond. Angel felt like a bit-player in a bad horror flick. His hand went to the thumb-break, retention strap on his holster, and he loosed his weapon without removing it.

With his hand on the butt of the pistol, he called, "Hello? Anybody home? State Police! Anybody here?"

He pushed the door open and a swarm of flies spilled from the house. Accompanying the flies, a singular, clearly identifiable odor erupted and tarred his senses: not just his sense of smell, but even taste and touch. The repulsive emanation seemed to coat him inside and out, and he stumbled back and vomited off the porch. The equally repulsive flies caused him to wave his arms around like a puppet on meth, as he tried to keep them from lighting on him. He spilled into the yard and staggered, doubled over, through the weeds to his cruiser. He put his left hand on the hot hood of the Crown Vic' for support and crossed himself with the other. He knew he had to go in, but he couldn't just yet. First he would call it in.

Angel's ordeal had started earlier that afternoon. Halfway through the second ring of the 911 switchboard, Rita dropped her emery board, clicked the answer button, and grabbed a ballpoint pen. She spoke into the mouthpiece of the hands-free headset that parted her hair from ear to ear and, with trained efficiency, extracted all the information she could. Whatever she needed to do to help the VA State Police to resolve a problem, she would do. She liked her job.

"I know she's away, but her car just went by," said a thin voice in Rita's earpiece.

It was a woman's voice, slow with the clarity of age, and she made no attempt to hide the antiquity of her diction. Maybe, after nearly a century of living, she knew of no better way to speak. Or perhaps she didn't know how much her manner of speech differed from that of younger generations.

"We'll have someone check it out," Rita responded.

Rita looked attractive in her crisp jacket, blouse and cream-colored slacks, and she took her job as dispatcher for the Virginia State Police seriously. She had completed a rigorous training program and accumulated years of experience; she approached her job with the attitude that she was an indispensable part of the Virginia law enforcement team, an insider in an exclusive world.

She immediately compared the caller ID information on the screen in front of her with the information the woman had given. Now she asked for and prepared to write down the name and location of the owner of the suspect vehicle. The caller, Esther Aubrey, didn't know the exact address of the owner, or the license number of the car. She didn't know the make or model, or the model year either, but she recognized the "dusty, old thing," and knew it belonged to Thelma Hardin; just an old, blue sedan that belonged to Thelma Hardin.

Esther had called the Virginia State Police because she didn't trust the Warren County Sheriff's Department to do anything about the possibly stolen car. To hear Esther tell it, they had ignored her in the past many times. Sometimes they told her she needed to call the Page County Sheriff or the Shenandoah County Sheriff, even though she didn't live in either of those counties. The truth of the matter was that her farmhouse sat in Warren County, two hundred yards from the corner where it joined the two other counties. Thelma Hardin lived just over the hill, but in Shenandoah County. Esther wasn't really clear on that; the lines were invisible except on maps, and she didn't use maps. But the State Police were professionals. Esther knew they would do something about the puzzling—and according to Esther—criminal activity.

If Rita had known how many false alarms Esther had raised in the past with local law enforcement jurisdictions, she may not have put quite so much effort into her reaction to the call. But Rita didn't know about the late night 'intruders' who turned out to be raccoons; or the neighbor who took down 'Esther's tree,' though it stood on his property. Rita treated her work as meticulously as she treated her appearance. She looked for and found the name Thelma Hardin in the Division of Motor Vehicles software on her computer.

According to the DMV, Thelma Hardin's rural address shared Esther Aubrey's zip code, despite lying in a different county. It seems the Postal Service didn't subscribe to the counties' idea of where lines should be drawn anymore than Esther did. Additionally, it said Thelma owned a dark blue, 1988 Chevy Lumina, and it gave the license plate number.

Rita requested the nearest State Trooper to respond and radioed the information.

"Ten-four."

Trooper Iglesias had reacted quickly. He used the opportunity to ease the big gray and blue Ford up to 100 mph on the mostly deserted I-66E. At mile marker ten, on a steamy, August Monday, rush hour had not yet invaded the interstate out this far.

Angel exited at exit thirteen, hung a left and reentered the highway heading in the opposite direction. He motored a few miles to a concrete surfaced superstructure and crossed the Shenandoah River. He left the highway at exit six and turned left on VA route 340 toward Front Royal. Angel slowed as he drove over the North Fork of the Shenandoah River and then over the South Fork, effectively re-crossing the river he had passed over on the interstate. The two branches had their confluence in Front Royal. From there the Shenandoah River flowed north, one of a minority of rivers in the world to flow in that direction. In Harper's Ferry, WV, it joined the Potomac River and flowed around mountains and over Great Falls into Washington, DC.

Angel drove quickly through the town of Front Royal, passing between gas stations, restaurants and a 7-11. Leaving town, he drove by the north entrance to Skyline Drive and the four lane divided highway became two lanes. Several miles later, he passed the Shenandoah River State Park, and ten miles from Front Royal, Angel arrived in Bentonville. The 16 foot canoe on a 30 foot high sign pole next to the post office distinguished Bentonville from most of the rest of the world. The canoe directed all comers and goers to the river rental outfitters down Acorn Hill.

Angel turned and drove past the chickens and goats in the mud pen on his right. What had once been a dirt road now unfurled in fresh asphalt, winding down through the woods and out into the bright sunlight by the river. He drove between canoe and tube rental shanties to the low-water bridge. When the river rose too far above its normal level, the bridge went under, but today it sat two feet above the river's surface, its single concrete lane baking in the hot sun. The guardrails were six-inch tall borders, more of a warning than a preventative. On the other side of the river, the road surface returned to Virginia dust on a bed of rock and clay, and Angel followed the meandering road through an area reminiscent of the scenery and banjo music in *Deliverance*. Angel put his hand on his pistol, affirming that he had not forgotten to bring it to work. Eventually he emerged in Fort Valley, in the Massanutten Mountains. A valley within the Shenandoah Valley, it lies between the two branches of the Shenandoah River surrounded by parts of the George Washington National Forest.

He savored being off the interstates and highways where he spent most of his time. There, the heat and hardness of the asphalt and concrete seemed contagious, tempering men to a callous loneliness. But out here, near the mountains and streams, life became robust and invigorating. The hills and valleys teemed with wildlife, from amphibious frogs and turtles to barking foxes, and cougars returning to their native habitat. Angel felt good just being in the country.

It's beautiful, he thought, *So much nicer than the dry plains in west Texas. It's so green!*

Angel Iglesias had come from Peru via El Paso, his father's chance destination after divorcing Angel's mother in Lima. Angel completed his education in Peru and then, at his mother's insistence, had joined his father in El Paso. Both of his parents, in a rare moment of agreement, wanted him to reap the benefits of life in the United States, or *America,* as they called it. An economy that left half the population with incomes below the poverty level hampered life in Peru.

Not long after Angel arrived in the US, he and his father moved east and settled in Virginia, but they had been in west Texas long enough for Angel to know he liked Virginia better. Fortunately, Señor Iglesias had met fellow Peruvians in Texas with relatives in the Washington, DC area. They told him of entire communities of Peruvians as well as other South Americans. He longed for the company of his fellow countrymen. They spoke and thought and lived differently from the Mexicans and other Central Americans in Texas. Besides, Northern Virginia teemed with opportunity.

Angel continued his search for Thelma Hardin's address. Fortunately for Rita, who continued to shape her nails, Esther Aubrey saw Angel go by and put her phone back in its cradle.

"It's about time," Esther told her fat, longhaired cat, who gave her a look that could have been mistaken for intelligent.

Angel found Thelma Hardin's place, an old farmhouse that sat thirsting for paint on a dirt road off another dirt road. It retained only traces of its former warmth and dignity on the grayed wooden construction, circa 1890. A ditch along the side of the road sunk, impassable except for a corroding, corrugated steel pipe with some dirt over it. The rest of the ditch acted as a weed-infested moat across the front of the unkempt acre, and sagging shutters further the aggravated house's lack of curb appeal. The previously green tin roof had surrendered to the slow burn of rust, leaving it mostly unsightly, ragged and brown.

Now he stood in the dirt in front of it wiping the spittle off his mouth. Yes, he would call it in before he went in. Or maybe he would just wait until the crime scene people arrived.

Chapter 1

Six hours earlier and sixty-five miles away from where Angel would stand in his own sickness in Thelma Hardin's yard, Morey Stenich, supervisor of collection and delivery at the Fairfax Post Office, languished in postal problems. A tray of mail containing several hundred social security checks addressed to residents in Fairfax ended up in the wrong post office. Someone working midnights at the Merrifield Sectional Center had looked at one zip code too many and sent a tray marked 22030 to the post office that served 22003. Hundreds of retirees in Fairfax would be waiting for checks that sat in a gray plastic tray in Annandale. Morey instructed his carriers to explain the situation if they had to, apologize, and assure anyone who asked that their check would be delivered tomorrow.

In addition to the problem of the misplaced checks, Morey needed to complete a 'driver observation report.' People with more authority than Morey demanded that he evaluate the driving habits of at least two letter carriers per week. That meant Morey had to follow someone around for a while and fill out a form, checking off things the driver did or didn't do correctly.

But, thought Morey, *I might be able to take advantage of this bit of work. I'll do the driver observation today and avoid all the complaints about the missing Social Security checks. Let the clerks take the phone calls.*

Most weeks Morey just invented the driver observation reports without leaving the air-conditioned office. He would simply put the name of someone currently in his favor at the top of the report, fill in his or her truck number, and pick a street on their route. Then, to show that they had delivered the mail safely, Morey put check marks in the correct boxes and wrote a flattering comment at the bottom of the page. Just to cover his butt, he would wait until the carrier came back in the afternoon and ask what time he or she had actually been on the street where Morey claimed to have seen them. Then he would fill in the time while they watched and hand them their copy. 'Nice job,' Morey would say, and they would both laugh. It was a win/win situation: Morey completed his report and his buddy got a good review.

But today he would do the report correctly and get away from the mail, the dust, and the impending complaints about the missing checks. Besides, he hadn't submitted an unfavorable driver observation report in at least a month, and he didn't want his superiors to think he would shirk his duty, even though he usually did. Morey believed the submission of unfavorable reports indicated his commitment and competence, sort of like ticket quotas for policemen. He made up his mind that someone had to receive a bad review today. And Jack Casey would make a nice stepping stone in his pathway to postal success.

While Morey planned to undermine Jack Casey's lackluster blue-collar career, Jack worked on getting his route ready to deliver. He spent half of every morning inside the Fairfax Post Office sorting mail and developing carpal and cubital tunnel problems. But the mail had to be in order, or delivery would be impossible.

After an oppressive three or four hours of focusing on names and addresses and putting each piece of mail in its proper slot, Jack pulled all the mail back out of the case. He set it in trays, all in the correct delivery sequence. Then he wheeled the entire route out to his vehicle, a 1994 Grumman, right-hand drive piece of junk. The trays of glossy magazines, advertisements and catalogues weighed up to 70 pounds, and they had to be placed in sequence in the truck. The parcels that wouldn't fit in trays had to be in some semblance of order, too, so that Jack could find them when he needed them.

This morning Jack's mail truck felt like a convection oven on wheels. A tiny fan, mounted on the dash, kept cutting on and off because dust and dirt caked the wiring and the switch. Additionally, the fan flopped around every time the truck moved. It had been whacked so many times by the heavy trays of mail that the abuse had stripped the threads of the thumbscrew that used to hold it in place.

Jack had a mirthless laugh reserved for his vocation. His career as a letter carrier had landed in his lap eighteen years ago, when he graduated from Paul VI High School in Fairfax. The school had opened three years before he entered the ninth grade as part of the Class of '91.

His parents were good Catholics, but despite their beliefs and practices, Jack remained an only child. Mom and Dad Casey raised him in their faith, but he lacked their conviction. He caved in to temptation every time it presented itself, starting with smoking cigarettes at age 11. At fourteen, he began consuming beer, at least on weekends, and soon it began consuming him. Shortly after his sixteenth birthday, Jack's father died. Someone shot him to death during a routine traffic stop. The driver had a trunk full of weapons and drugs, and he shot Jack's father before he could even ask to see his license and registration. Officer Casey bled to death on the pavement, leaving Jack and his mother to fend for themselves.

Jack's mother, Eileen, worked hard running an office for a house cleaning service, and she did the best she could with a child full of angst over losing his father. She never remarried. She spent the rest of her short life working to support Jack and filling him with quotes from the bible and from the saints of the Catholic Church. Jack could still hear her voice in his head saying, *It's better to give than to receive*, or, *Do unto others, as you would have them do unto you.*

Despite her best efforts, at sixteen, after his father died, Jack quit attending Mass. When he graduated from Paul VI High School, he wanted to get high more than he wanted to go to college or learn a trade, so he took the test for postal employment. It seemed like an easy solution to the money thing. After a few months of riotous living, a letter arrived enjoining him to start the employment process. He got the job. It paid well, especially for a nineteen-year-old with no bills. He found that, even after hours of drudgery at the post office, he still had the energy to engage in excessive overindulgence. Sex, alcohol and drugs fed his desires. Early in his drinking career, he enjoyed a high tolerance for alcohol, and his 'friends' who tried to keep up with his intake envied him. They called him their designated drunken driver because, except for Jack, none of them could still function by the end of the night.

Life is good, he thought.

After eight years of postal drudgery during the day and immoderate self indulgence at night, Jack married Carla, a good woman, forgiving and free, intelligent, helpful, and deserving of someone who behaved better than Jack. He loved her, but by now addiction to alcohol ruled his life. Six years after marrying Carla, Jack's mother died of cancer, and Jack went on a bender that never seemed to end. Carla left him a few months after that. The shock of total aloneness caused him to change, but not soon enough to save his marriage.

Now, 37 years old and four years into divorce and sobriety, he sat in an aluminum box with a seat and steering wheel, surrounded by trays of mail. The truck didn't have air conditioning, and the fan flopped around like a broken wrist. Nor did it have a radio to help divert his attention from the torrid summer heat. Unlike private companies, the Postal Service didn't allow drivers the luxury of a radio, even if they brought their own: too distracting. It reminded Jack of high school and his mother telling him he couldn't have the stereo on while he did his homework.

But Jack owned up to his mistakes and remained philosophical about his job. He would survive. He occupied his off time with things that interested him, like reading and fishing. He learned what he could about home repair and remodeling and also about auto maintenance and repair. He enjoyed life despite what he had and hadn't made of it.

This morning at only 10:30, Jack headed for his first delivery already dripping with sweat. His light blue, polyester shirt with the eagle on the sleeve showed growing patches of dampness, not only under his arms, but also on the front and back. He knew the wetness would soon spread to his blue gray shorts. Even his socks were soggy.

Jack drove to his route without breaking too many laws. The sooner he started his deliveries, the sooner he would finish, and he already wanted out of the heat.

He started in a relatively new neighborhood, and the first few deliveries went off quickly. Then, in a cul-de-sac with curbside boxes, Jack pulled up to a mailbox and slammed the mail truck into park. He pulled back the sliding door and walked rapidly toward the house, carrying a package too large to fit in the mailbox. The new neighborhood offered no protection from the summer sun, just the token twigs the developer had planted. Someday, years from now, maples would cool the yards, but until then they remained scorched sod.

At least it's a small package, Jack thought.

He recalled the fifty-pound leaf springs for a pick-up truck someone had ordered through a catalogue. Jack had to leave his route to help Joanne, on the route next to his, deliver them to a third-floor walk-up apartment. Big business knew the easiest and cheapest way to get their freight hauled: just mail it.

Today, to his relief, he didn't have to deliver any leaf springs. He placed the little package behind a terracotta pot full of pansies on a concrete slab and rang the doorbell at the front door. Without waiting for anyone to answer, he turned and walked back to his mail truck. He pulled halfway around the cul-de-sac without looking back, so he didn't see Morey's dull black Toyota Corolla at the curb two houses behind. Its motor ran quietly, supplementing the heat of the already sweltering August morning. After Jack accelerated to the next mailbox, he shoved the mail in, shut the box and nearly pulled away before he noticed the black car jerk to a stop behind him. He watched in the mirror as the door opened and the ugly driver struggled out. Jack considered pulling to the next box. And then he could do it again each time Morey got out!

I wonder how many deliveries I can make before he honks his horn. Jack thought. And then he thouht, *Nah. There's got to be at least one adult in the playground.*

Morey scurried around the front of his Toyota and disappeared momentarily behind the mail truck, only to reappear on the driver's side, the right-hand side of Jack's delivery vehicle. He began scribbling on his clipboard, entirely too busy to notice Jack's amusement.

Jack looked down at Morey and thought about giving him a pat on the head, but he didn't.

Do unto others, Jackie. Remember the Golden Rule.

I will, Mom, Jack thought, *But just for you.*

Jack and Morey didn't entertain any friendly feelings, and lately a little animosity had arisen. When Morey first transferred to the Fairfax Post Office as the new delivery supervisor, Jack worked hard for him. He would have for anybody. If not her faith, Jack had at least adopted his mother's work ethic, and it wouldn't allow him to do otherwise. It didn't take long, however, for Morey's lack of management skills and lack of integrity to become apparent. Jack survived a gut-wrenching divorce and a necessary sabbatical from alcohol, but he had no tolerance for Morey's vaporous drivel or his duplicity. In a few short weeks after Morey's arrival, Jack's intuitive reflex toward him had hardened, and soon, the brittle working relationship shattered. Any former sentiments evaporated.

But Jack's mother had taught him to treat others kindly, or at least not unkindly, so as Morey continued to scribble, Jack said, "What's up, Morey?"

"I'm writing you up," Morey blustered as he cradled his clipboard in his arm.

Jack suppressed a laugh as he conjured an image of Morey skulking around, 'writing people up,' in his black shirt and cartoon-character tie (the same tie postal clerks tried to hawk over the counter, the one with the Warner Brothers stamps on it).

Jack felt more pity for Morey than hatred, but he couldn't help reacting to the overbearing attempt at authority.

"Write me up for what, Morey?" Jack asked. "The Roberts want their packages left on the porch."

Jack assumed leaving the package had drawn Morey's attention. The rulebook said something like knock on the door, wait, knock again, wait, and then write a notice, leave it in the mailbox, and take the package back to the post office. That meant the Roberts would have to drive to the post office to pick up the package, if they got home from work before the post office closed. Actually, the Roberts had spoken to Jack about the inconvenience and asked him to leave their packages on their porch. Technically, Jack needed the request in writing in the 'special orders' section of his route book, but no one ever looked there anyway.

"You were driving with your door open and no seat belt on," Morey shot back.

Jack ignored those two rules as soon as he got off the highway. He needed to get in and out of the truck pretty often while he delivered mail and the quicker the better in this heat.

Jack made a stab at defending himself just because he thought he should; he didn't really think it would change anything.

"Morey, it's less than 80 feet between these mailboxes, and I wasn't even going ten miles per hour. Didn't you tell us you weren't going sweat the small stuff?"

"I don't think you'll be able to get any witnesses to me saying that."

Morey didn't look up or even stop writing and his contemptuous reply and odious exhalation seemed to hang in the humidity between him and Jack.

Jack's ire surfaced. He gave no thought to winning the war between himself and Morey. In the heat of the moment, he would win the battle.

"Well, in that case, Morey, I think you're a depraved moral degenerate, a liar and a pompous ass, and I don't think you have any witnesses to me saying that."

As Morey's head jerked up at the insult, Jack slammed the contentious open door in his face. The result left Jack exposed from the knees up; the top half of the door consisted of a window big enough to fall out of. Nothing stood between him and Morey other than contempt, but Jack acted as if Morey didn't exist and took the time to fasten his lap belt. Morey's Warner Brothers tie accurately accented the scene: "Th-th-th that's all folks!" it seemed to say. Jack pulled away without laughing, but he wanted to.

Morey stood in the road, seething in the August steam, watching Jack pull away.

Morey wasn't lying about the witnesses. His so-called friends would back him up, and the rest of the carriers didn't want to deal with the strain of getting on his bad side. Sometimes Morey spent more time getting even than he did supervising.

Chapter 2

Jack finished his deliveries in the new subdivision with its dull and unimaginative landscape, turned a corner and entered a different world. He felt the average household income drop like the stock market on a bad day. People on this street lived on less than half of what people in the new neighborhood lived on. He drove for one block and parked near the intersection of Maple and Hill. Residents on Maple Street, as in all the old neighborhoods in Fairfax, still enjoyed mail delivery to their doors. The Postal Service would have changed that, but orders from above prevented it.

Jack would walk the rest of his route. From where he parked, he could deliver down one side of the block of Maple Street, and double-back on the other. When he returned to his truck, he could refill his mailbag and deliver a block of Hill Street. Parked at an intersection as he was, he could deliver in four directions before moving the truck up a couple of blocks. It took less than an hour on a good day, but today didn't qualify as a good day.

Today the heat index hit 102°F, and by the time Jack delivered mail to a block of houses and returned to the closed-up truck, the temperature inside hit 115°F.

In addition to the heat, Jack had to deal with an increasing number of people waiting for their missing social security checks. Mostly old people populated old neighborhoods. But at least he would be out of the oven-like vehicle for a little while, and the trees, as mature as the residents, shaded and cooled the grassy lawns.

Maple Street had come to life long before Jack got there. Much earlier that morning, Sandi Andersen shed the too-large, white T-shirt she slept in as she dragged her feet down the hallway of her rented, antiquated bungalow. Appropriately, a large maple tree shaded the entire front yard, as well as the unpaved driveway, or, more correctly, the two graveled ruts with grass growing between them.

Sandi had signed a lease a year and a half ago, but ten months later, Race Hardin moved in with her. Living with Race made life much easier. She had more money and a better car, a much better car. Great sex also enhanced the arrangement. He always made love to her like he had something to prove. She used words to encourage his feelings of inadequacy and then enjoyed his best attempts at overcoming them. 'No, not yet,' she would say, or 'Now, Race, do it now!' She had trained him well.

While Race and two friends left for work, Sandi dragged her T-shirt on the floor behind her. Actually, it belonged to Race. It proclaimed boldly in loud colors, his proclivity for drunkenness and sexy women in a particular Nags Head, North Carolina bar. Sandi shambled naked into the bedroom and stood for a moment in front of the full-length mirror on the closet door. A sexy image of her 32-year-old form reflected back at her, and, though it would never appear on the glossy cover of a magazine, it endowed her with all the seductive allurement she would need in life. Her body curved where it should, and exemplified balance: no feature too big, no feature too small; a tribute to symmetry.

Race Hardin, she thought, *you're a lucky man.*

She laughed as she ran the shower, recalling the last five minutes, when she leaned in the doorway at the front of the house. Five steps climbed to the stoop, where she stood and waved as Race climbed into George Reiss's pick-up truck. George sat in the driver's seat, and another man, Eddie Hackley, slid to the middle of the seat to make room for Race. Eddie tried to ogle Sandi while he slid over. Race's over-sized T-shirt made up her only visible attire, and Eddie hoped she would wave her hand just a little higher. He couldn't overcome his compulsion to leer, even in the presence of her lover. But, as she leaned on the door jam, her left elbow remained cupped in her right hand, and the bottom of the shirt continued to cover her torso, though not by much.

"See anything you like, Eddie?" Race inquired as he swung into the truck.

Race derived a sadistic pleasure from teasing Eddie, though he pitied him more than anything else. Short and skinny, Eddie didn't possess the strength, stamina or physical presence of Race or George. Eddie, who was thin from not eating and wrinkled from smoking, looked much older than Race, even though they were the same age—28. Most people would have guessed him closer to George's age—56.

"S-Sure," Eddie stammered. "I like Sandi alright."

Eddie's ears turned red. George smirked, while Race laughed out loud at Eddie.

Sandi smiled as she stood in the doorway waving and enjoying the discomfort she caused, and she watched as the three of them left.

While Sandi lathered herself in the shower, George's old pick-up moved slowly down the quiet street. He drove to where Maple Street collided with a five-lane riot of cars, traffic signals, fast food restaurants, and gas stations. Two lanes traveled east, two lanes traveled west, and the middle lane of Lee Highway served as an awkward mesh of the crowded thoroughfare, allowing traffic from either direction to attempt a left turn through the oncoming hordes. But just before George reached the turbulent intersection, he slipped into the side entrance of a convenience store parking lot.

"Don't forget, it's Monday," Race said to George as the men piled out of the truck. "Get the numbers.

Inside the store George and Race poured fresh coffee, standing elbow to elbow with other mostly blue-collar workers. Occasionally, suit and tie guys showed up, always late for something, always in a hurry, usually bleary-eyed from working late or drinking late or staying up late with wives or girlfriends or both. A few women came in, mostly looking like office workers and in a hurry like their tie wearing counterparts. Once in a while, though, women came in wearing work boots, dressed in denim and stained T-shirts. They worked in warehouses or manufacturing plants, or they held flags at road construction sites. Some drove dump trucks. A few were dressed in uniform, military or law enforcement personnel.

The men that worked outdoors, the ones that spent their blood and sweat to make a living, men like George, Race and Eddie, never rushed, especially in August. Sweat would soak them soon enough, if it hadn't already.

George placed a lid on his steaming cup and got in line. At the register, he picked up a printout of the winning lottery numbers from the weekend drawing. As George walked out, Race got a breakfast sandwich to go with his coffee. Eddie followed with a cold case of a generic beer. It was cheap.

♠

After showering, Sandi applied a little make-up to her already attractive face, and caressed some gel into her clipped, blonde hair. She slipped her arms into a gossamer camisole, knowing it would be visible through the blouse of her uniform. Her job required a uniform, but she didn't mind. She looked good in the dark blue slacks and the crisp white blouse. The brass-colored nametag made her look official.

This should be a flight attendant's uniform, she told herself for the thousandth time. *One lousy inch too short and I'm condemned to the ticketing counter, part of the ground crew: no glamour and lower pay.*

She stopped herself before she got carried away. This particular resentment had consumed her whenever she let it, usually once a day, sometimes more than that.

I've gotta get going, she thought, *I don't want to miss another employee-integrity meeting.*

She worked for an airline that prided itself on retaining scrupulous employees, and she would have to listen to the drivel, no matter how she felt about it.

Sandi hopped in her used, but new to her, Porsche Boxster and accelerated out of the neighborhood. She wheeled her German engineered machine onto route 50 going west out of Fairfax, the same road Race, George and Eddie had taken earlier. The Porsche demonstrably out-performed George's GMC pick-up, as well as most of the other cars sharing her commute. She had owned the sports car for just a couple of months, and she loved it. Zipping past slower drivers, she changed lanes as often as she wanted, and while she attacked the traffic, she juggled figures in her head. She wanted to pay off the Porsche.

If I had just a little more income, she whispered, unaware that her lips were moving and her voice was audible.

But it didn't matter; no one else could have heard her. She occupied that secret place where drivers go, living as though invisible in the midst of rush hour traffic. Even if someone had heard her, the thought of 'a little more income' would be nothing new. Everyone around her had become engrossed in the idea at one time or another. But if she could pay off the Porsche, that car payment would become disposable income.

An extra $650 a month! I could do plenty with that.

Sharing living expenses with Race had improved her standard of living, but not enough to quench her thirst for more. Besides, Sandi knew that her present temporary circumstance wouldn't last long. She had terminated past entanglements as soon as they became a burden, and the conclusions weren't always peaceful. Her most promising beau chose to study music, even though he had the mental capacity for medicine and had been accepted at the Duke University School of Medicine. When he revealed his decision she upbraided him on the spot, and she had never spoken to him again. But that happened years ago. Time to enhance her life closed in on her. Unless Race struck out on his own and began building homes or making money in real estate, she wouldn't keep him around much longer.

I don't need kids or permanence, Sandi told herself. *I need to quit working and start living the way I want to.*

Her thoughts of Race vacillated as she drove past the very spot where he and she had met a little over a year ago. He had been driving north on Route 28 to a job site in Herndon, and she had come up the ramp from Route 50 to go in the same direction. As she came up the ramp Race drove into her blind spot. She didn't see him, and he didn't anticipate her sudden merge. The ensuing collision, more a clip than a crash, frightened her, and it got his adrenaline flowing. They both pulled over.

"I'm so sorry!" Sandi said when they met behind her car. "I didn't see you there; I just changed lanes! Are you all right?" She was shaken and frightened, standing in front of a young, muscular construction worker who stood head and shoulders above her.

Race had hopped from his truck and approached her car ready for an altercation, but his mood and humor changed the moment he saw her. Suddenly being late for work, getting a ticket, and maybe having to get his truck repaired became less important than impressing the petite, attractive daughter of Eve in front of him.

"Yeah, I'm fine. Are *you* okay?" he asked.

To him she seemed like a little lamb, trembling and more frightened than hurt. His fostering instinct surfaced, something he rarely allowed, and he wanted to take care of her. And at that moment, she wanted to be taken care of.

"I think so," she said.

A Fairfax county cruiser with blue lights flashing from the rack on top pulled in behind them, thankfully, without the blaring siren and series of startling noises that sometimes accompanied the arrival of the police. A stocky, uniformed officer climbed out, shrinking from the four lanes of traffic now slowing to a crawl beside him. As he approached Sandi and Race, he looked mainly for signs of injury, but he also wanted to keep the rush hour traffic moving. He made sure neither vehicle blocked the road. After a brief explanation from Race, he decided not to ticket him for hitting her car in the rear or to ticket Sandi for an illegal lane change.

"Just one of those things," Race said, and added, "I don't think my truck got damaged."

Seeing only minimal damage to Sandi's car and ascertaining that both drivers were licensed and insured, he left them alone to exchange information. He walked back to his cruiser and removed some flares from the trunk to warn the oncoming traffic of the slowdown. Sandi and Race exchanged insurance information and would be gone long before the flares burned out.

That evening Race phoned Sandi. After a short conversation about the fender bender, they continued to talk for over an hour, sharing their thoughts and aspirations with each other, but not their secrets, at least not all of them. After that, Race began picking up Sandi and taking her to work while her second-hand Mitsubishi underwent repairs. The carpooling led to dating, and within four months Race had moved into the bungalow in Fairfax. Benefits included a shorter commute for him, less rent to pay for her, and great sex. They rarely had any deep discussions, so they rarely had any disagreement. They enjoyed a mutually beneficial relationship.

But Sandi knew their relationship lacked at least one element: financial independence, or, better still, decadent wealth. Between her income and Race's prospects, would they have enough money for her to live the way she intended to live?

I don't think so! she thought.

Chapter 3

By the time Sandi finished dressing for work, George, Eddie and Race had driven out of Fairfax and past Arcola. Between George's coffee stirring, Race's junk food eating, and Eddie's morning beer drinking, they hadn't thought to check their lottery tickets against the winning numbers.

When Eddie had finally consumed enough to stop his morning tremors, he garbled, "Lemme see those tickis." He had just finished his third beer, and, in his advanced state of dipsomania, three were enough for the effects of the alcohol to become apparent. His addiction had reached a stage of lowered tolerance, and eventually, if he didn't do something about it, it would kill him, probably slowly. Right now, though, in his current state of cheap euphoria, he felt lucky.

Race, in response to Eddie's drunken request for the tickets, reached for his wallet, and nearly clobbered Eddie with his elbow. Eddie never even flinched, not so much because he had no fear, but more because he was too slow to react.

From this point in the day, Eddie would deteriorate in direct proportion to the accumulation of empty cans on the floor of George's truck. Depending on Eddie's ability at the end of the day, George would make him pick them up, though many evenings George just poured Eddie out at his house and picked up the cans himself. He had hired Eddie as a helper many years ago when the beer consumption had been less out of control, but Eddie had evolved from helper to an adopted care project. George wouldn't fire him, even though he knew he should.

"Here, Mister Money," Race said, handing Eddie the tickets. "Tell me we won."

And so began the Monday morning ritual. Race would say, 'Tell me we won,' like someone might say, 'Show me the money.' Next Eddie would check the three tickets against the winning numbers and after the third one he would say, 'We won!' only they hadn't. Winning the lottery didn't happen to three construction workers on their way to work, even if those three guys bought three tickets every Friday and were still young enough to enjoy the booty. That only happened to other people, people you never met, but occasionally you heard about on the news or read about in the paper. Old people won, too late in life to make it worthwhile. What a waste! Still, the men put up a buck apiece every Friday and checked their three tickets on Monday to see if they were new millionaires. Race held the tickets over the weekend, but he and George and Eddie had an unwritten agreement: all three tickets belonged to the group; whatever they won, they split. So far, after nine months of pooling their money, the winnings had only amounted to five dollars, twice, and four free tickets on four different Mondays.

George handed Eddie the winning numbers, and Eddie checked the first ticket against them. Then he handed the ticket to Race. He knew better than to tear it up or throw it out. Someone with more functioning brain cells had to double-check the numbers before discarding the ticket. Eddie checked the second ticket and laid it in Race's hand on top of the first. Now George and Race braced themselves for the victory yell as Eddie held the last ticket next to the winning numbers. The counterfeit exuberance that inevitably accompanied the phony, winning announcement, sometimes ended in spilt beer.

This morning though, after too long a pause, Eddie said, "We won."

He said it quietly, with a hint of wonder, as if he had just found out you can't sail off the edge of the earth.

"C'mon," Race chided, "put a little *umph* into it."

George chuckled, about as close as he got to a laugh these days. A lifetime of hard work had made him a solemn, though not unhappy, man.

"I'm serious," Eddie said, "We won." His slurred speech had disappeared and he sounded like a boy. He turned to Race with his mouth open, unconsciously offering the ticket and the paper with the winning numbers on it.

George glanced at Race and raised an eyebrow. Race glanced back at him and took the two pieces of paper from Eddie.

"If this isn't a winner, Eddie, I'm shoving the rest of that case of beer up your ass, one can at a time."

Race tossed off the physically impossible epithet as if afflicted with Tourette's. It had become habit, not even a bad one by his estimation. He used foul language often; it served a variety of purposes. At the moment, he was making sure that Eddie knew who commanded the dominant role between them.

Race checked the ticket numbers against the winning numbers. He double-checked the last ticket Eddie had handed him.

"Damn!" he said. "Pull over, George, there!" and he pointed, nearly hitting Eddie in the face with his forearm.

George hit the brakes and hung a hard left onto a dirt road outside of Arcola. The squealing tires, blaring horn and the obscene gesture from the driver behind him faded, lost in the billowing dust and the rattle of tools as George's truck bounced over a few potholes. George slowed down on the narrow road and drove straight ahead for about a hundred yards where the road ended in a little dirt circle in the woods. Fishermen would sometimes park there and walk to the Beaver Dam Reservoir, but this morning George, Eddie and Race had the place to themselves. After all, on Mondays most people were at work.

Race compared the ticket to the printout for a third time, checking each number carefully.

"Look at this, George," Race said as he handed him the two pieces of paper.

After a moment George said, "Well, sheeyit...looks like a match to me." His own voice startled him as he asked, "How much did we win?"

He looked at Eddie for some reason, assuming that the first person to discover the matching numbers would know.

"I dunno…" Eddie managed, staring at the ticket in George's hand, as if it would tell him the answer.

Then they both looked at Race.

"Eleven million dollars," said Race, locking eyes with George. "The immediate payoff should be about 5½, million. After taxes, 2½, maybe 3, million?"

"That's about a million dollars apiece," said George.

Eddie's hand shook as he lifted another can of Milwaukee's Best to his mouth. It clattered against his teeth.

A million bucks give or take a couple hundred thousand George thought.

George had married Ellen right out of high school. He had been a young buck with a good heart; she had been an attractive girl, not sophisticated or drop-dead gorgeous, but pretty in a healthy sort of way; and she and George shared the same kindhearted temperament. Their love for each other had lasted forty years, and, despite a few wrinkles, it remained as strong as ever; in fact, it had grown stronger. They were a rare couple. Two people who had married best friends and were still best friends.

They met in the high school gym at a sock hop in the early sixties. Songs like *Our Day Will Come* and *Chapel of Love* had kept them in each other's arms the entire night. George's pomaded hair and rolled-up short sleeves gave him a Jerry Lee Lewis look, The Killer, and Ellen's dark hair swirled with her knee-length, pleated skirt as they danced. They had slipped out the side door early in the evening and shared a few sips of stolen bourbon from a classmate's flask. Then they slipped out later, when no one was there, and shared their first kiss.

That pretty much sealed the deal, George liked to say.

Love and then marriage had come easy for them, and in their passion Ellen had given birth to three children. Grown and on their own now, the kids stayed close, geographically and in thought and by telephone.

George and Ellen found contentment in the house they had purchased thirty-two years ago, despite the quiet without little ones and then teenagers around. They had never quite gotten used to that. Still, it had been home for more years than either one of them had ever lived in one place before. Their three bedroom brick rambler had been built in the '50's and had the same floor plan as every other house on the street. They all had flat picture windows in front, too, but George had replaced theirs with a bay window to create a subtle distinction between their house and the rest on the block. And now, with the nest empty, Ellen had a sewing room just for sewing, and they had a guestroom.

The mortgage payment had relinquished its death grip on the budget two years ago, and George's wages were higher now. He and Ellen were comfortable. George contracted smaller construction jobs, no longer caught in the trap of trading time, energy and his life's blood for money. He worked fewer hours than when he was younger, and took on fewer projects than before. He finally had some time to spend with Ellen, and they planned to retire as soon as he reached sixty-two. He could claim a reduced amount of Social Security and why shouldn't he? He figured the break-even point between smaller payment now and a higher one later was way down the road.

At fifty-eight, retirement looked just a quick four years away. But not now, not with this lottery ticket in his hand! Now George couldn't wait to tell Ellen that they had won. A million dollars in addition to their savings meant immediate retirement.

"Hell, I'd be crazy not to," he told Race and Eddie, sitting in the truck in the dirt lot near the reservoir.

He couldn't stop smiling.

"I gotta pee," he said and almost laughed for the second time that morning as he got out and walked to the back of the truck.

"We can buy a house " Eddie exclaimed. "And a good car, or maybe a pick-up, yeah, a new one."

Eddie Spechi and Sharyl had met in high school like George and Ellen, though neither of them graduated. Their first kiss had been in the back seat of Eddie's rusty Pontiac Catalina. He introduced Sharyl to the headiness of intoxication and the cost of unprotected sex in the same night. They were expecting by the time Eddie was in his second year of the eleventh grade. A sixteen-year-old sophomore, Sharyl dropped out of high school to have their first child. Eddie quit school, too, and got a job as a laborer at a construction site. He drank all the time, even back then, and for a while Sharyl tried to keep up. Now, eleven years later, Eddie still worked for someone else. George graciously allowed him the title 'carpenter,' though by the end of any given day, Eddie's qualifications had degenerated to that of an unskilled laborer, and not a very good one. Sharyl had given up drinking and tried to maintain a decent home for the family which now included three children, but mostly she failed. Life proved too much for her alone, and Eddie had become more of a burden than a help.

They lived in a tiny, old, rented, two-story townhouse in a neighborhood where young couples like George and Ellen had started their journeys in life, but Eddie and Sharyl had never moved up. They started at the bottom and continued to wallow there.

But not anymore, Eddie thought.

He believed money, not sobriety, would solve their problems; and it *would* solve a lot of them. Sharyl would agree. He knew she would, and she would be thrilled. Unfortunately, money wouldn't solve their important problems, like caring for their children, themselves and each other.

"Yeah, we can buy a house," Eddie said, and slammed another half a can of beer.

Race just looked at Eddie and grinned. He had plans, too, but they weren't anyone else's business.

John Racine Hardin had been born in Racine, Wisconsin twenty-eight years ago. His mother, Thelma Hardin, had given him Racine for a middle name. She called him Race, and the nickname stuck. Her family name, Hardin, never changed. She never married Race's father or anyone else; no one had ever asked. Besides, Race's paternity remained uncertain. She didn't know for sure which of her sex partners had gotten her pregnant. Unlike George and Ellen or even Eddie a Sharyl, Thelma shared carnal knowledge with just about anyone who had the appetite, which included just about every guy she met. Not particularly pretty but pretty easy, kept her in boyfriends. When she became pregnant, 'who's yer daddy' became a multiple choice question ending in 'maybe all of the above.' Pregnant in a pre-DNA testing and pre-abortion (or not easy, anyway) world, she left Wisconsin in shame and came to Virginia.

She moved in with her aunt, a widow living on social security and egg money from her laying hens. Thelma and her baby lived upstairs in the old wooden farmhouse. Within two years the aunt died and Thelma's mother, the nearest surviving relative, inherited the property. She let Thelma live there free. Eventually she succumbed to cancer and a broken heart. Thelma inherited the farmhouse and owned the place, unencumbered.

Her job at Rootie's, a bar in Luray, paid enough to cover a baby sitter, utilities, food and little more, but it also afforded her the opportunity to meet men. She stayed socially active with booze, pills, and a series of so-called uncles, while Esther, the sixty-year-old woman who lived one farm over, babysat Race. Thelma loved Race, but not enough to give up her selfish desires. She didn't do her best to raise him.

When Race reached the age of four, Thelma, in an alcohol and drug induced haze had shared him with one of the perverts she occasionally brought home. He hadn't known enough to be afraid. His mother and her 'friend' had coddled him and fondled him in their bed. Everyone had their clothes off. He was just trying to be 'a good boy' when they started to hurt him. His mother comforted him, but it still hurt. Finally they let him go and he ran to his bedroom.

After what seemed a long time, his mother came for him and took him to the bathroom and cleaned him. He bled a little, but she told him it would be okay. She seemed frightened. She shook him and told him not to say anything or someone would take him away. Or did she say someone would take her away? He couldn't remember anymore. Nor could he remember exactly what had happened, and, though the atrocity continued for two more years, it remained buried in his psyche.

As Race grew, he got hit a lot—spanked, slapped, punched, kicked, shoved—he just seemed to be in the way. When he grew older, he found himself shoved out of the house and locked out: "Adults need their privacy." He saw his mother knocked around nearly as often as he had been. Sometimes, alone with his mother, she spoke to him, but not to guide him or to love him; she bewailed her own plight. When he got in trouble, which became more and more frequent, she didn't admonish or correct him; instead, she blamed him for bringing the bitterness and anguish of the world to her door and intruding upon her life.

He loved his mother because he knew no other, but he hated her, too.

At the age of nine, Race took a paper route and walked it most of the time. Sometimes he could borrow a bike. When he finally saved enough money to buy his own bicycle, Bill Zeke, the 'uncle' of that particular phase in his mother's life, took the money away and spent it on booze and lottery tickets. He told Race that a man has to fight to get anything in life, unless there was a stupid kid around who didn't know you had to fight to keep it as well.

"And let this be a lesson to you!"

He walked away laughing.

Race saved more money, but he kept it hidden. The next time the drunken Uncle Zeke demanded cash, little Race ran. Then, later, when Race got bigger and Uncle Zeke came at him for money, Race stood his ground. The encounter proved fast and ferocious, and the outcome gratifying. Race kept his money and Bill Zeke kept his distance. Race had learned a lesson of dubious value. After that, he swore to himself he would never run again or let anyone take what belonged to him.

In school, bullies learned to leave him alone. He never backed down, whether outnumbered or outsized. He fought like a cat; no rules existed in a confrontation with Race. The few who bested him regretted trying.

Eventually Race matured, at least physically. And he didn't suffer from the weakness of empathy, which kept most people from beating other human beings senseless over minor disagreements. He had put up with hurt and shame; they could, too. He fought to keep what little he had, and occasionally he fought to take what he couldn't get any other way. Uncle Zeke had taught him well.

Race remained unhampered by childhood friends, High School sweethearts and old college roommates. He used people. Now, sitting in

SOCIAL INSECURITY

George's truck in a dirt lot in the woods, the fighting could end. He would have more money than he ever imagined, enough to last the rest of his life. Just one skirmish remained.

Chapter 4

Jack turned the corner onto Maple Street and drove a block up the road. He parked where Maple crossed Pine and loaded his next bundle of magazines, newspapers and advertisements into his mailbag. The new pouches were blue canvass bags, but Jack still used an old leather bag, the kind of satchel the post office issued years ago, in the 'good ol' days.'

Nowadays it seemed problems at the post office surfaced daily, unlike in the early years, and employees handled their problems in various ways. Some worried, some complained, and a few 'went postal.' Others considered the bureaucratic tripe a form of entertainment. Jack did, and his mood had brightened since this morning's confrontation with Morey. It felt good to say what he thought, even though he knew it would cost him. Morey would retaliate, but so what. Let him play his imperious role.

Morey, in his confusion, tried to dictate attitudes instead of encouraging or inspiring people. He didn't know the postal service wanted him to supervise the collection and delivery of the mail, not badger and punish its employees. Carriers with years of experience and a good record didn't really need someone telling them what to do every micro moment of the day, but they got it anyway. There always seemed to be someone like Morey, who craved fear and subservience from his underlings.

Dull and institutionalized, Morey couldn't appreciate the lesson behind today's psychological trouncing. In his mind, respect and approval had nothing to do with the job. He was a bureaucratic ladder-climber who had no regard for his employees or the people they served.

Morey thought Jack was insubordinate and just wouldn't submit to authority, that he was a troublemaker.

Jack stepped out of his mail truck on Maple Street and locked it, but not because he thought Morey still lurked around the corner and might catch him violating another regulation. He locked it because delivering mail to Maple Street on foot would take him away from the truck leaving it vulnerable to thieves and vandals. He had no way of knowing who might happen by and grab a tray just to rifle the contents. It could contain cash, checks or credit cards; it might even contain bank records and social security numbers. Jack didn't want to cause any distress by negligence on his part. Life threw enough curves at you without help from the post office.

After locking the truck, Jack started walking back in the direction he had just driven; he headed for the first house on his right, the first of 23 houses on this particular block. Twelve houses lined the even side of the street and thirteen lined the odd, the disparity owing to a slight curve in the road. Not so much of a curve that you couldn't see the whole block, end to end, but enough that one extra house fit on the longer side. Jack delivered mail up one side and down the other, ending across the street from his truck. Then he refilled his pouch and headed off in the other direction.

He was in an old neighborhood where older people lived, and the number of social security recipients per household skyrocketed. As he progressed, some of the retired residents on the street met him at their mailboxes anticipating their checks. They were supposed to be delivered on the third of the month, and all the recipients knew it. The bold lettering on the front of the envelopes said so. Unfortunately, this was one of the few months in a lifetime that it wasn't going to happen. Not since that ill-fated tray had gone to Annandale.

So far, Jack had only had to explain the situation once, but it hadn't gone well:

"It says right on the envelope it'll be here on the third of the month, and now you tell me it'll be here tomorrow! Why should I believe *you*? How do I know you didn't lose it or deliver it to someone else?"

Jack ran out of time and answers and had to tell the old guy to call Morey, which wouldn't go over well, especially after the earlier run-in. Not only would Morey have to handle the complaint, the guy complaining now had the internal number to the Fairfax Post Office, not the 1-800 number. That would surely come up in Morey's next rant.

Just knowing he didn't have the anticipated retirement checks left Jack apprehensive, carrying an extra burden of anxiety along with the mail. He didn't want the people to think he had screwed up when he hadn't. He also didn't like being unable to deliver something he was supposed to have. Maybe that stemmed from his Mom's 'Do unto others...' maxim, or maybe he was just tired of disappointing people.

His years of alcoholic drinking had led to insane behavior, and Jack had shattered the hopes of those dearest to him. He didn't want to do that anymore, to anyone. Sometimes he carried an irrational sense of responsibility for other people's feelings.

Jack had delivered this route for years, and he knew which houses were supposed to receive a social security check. Every time he approached one of them and didn't have the check, he almost tip-toed, hoping no one was home. It was an irritating distraction, wondering when the next confrontation would be. He had no hand in the missing checks, but he was on the front line, and he was certain to take the blame. The complaints were sure to come, and most people were dead certain it was the mailman's fault.

Sometimes the complaints were about previous problems, trying to make a case for constant bad service, and it didn't matter if the problems had occurred last week or last century. Elephants and fixed-income retirees never forget. 'This isn't the first time this has happened,' they would grumble, never admitting that this was only the second time, and that the first time it happened was twenty years ago. Nor would they admit that the previous problem occurred in a town where they used to live. If the postal supervisor taking the call didn't get all the facts, which happened about 75 percent of the time, the carrier got the blame. It was unwritten postal code: the carrier is guilty until proven innocent. After all, if they are supposed to be working and you can't see them, they must be doing something wrong. That was the unofficial but working line of thinking at the post office.

Maybe I picked the wrong day to mess with Morey, Jack thought, though not without some amusement.

And even as he entertained the regret, Jack approached another beneficiary's house for which he had no check.

Maybe no one is home, he told himself, and not for the first time.

Usually at this particular house, on weekdays anyway, his wish would be granted. A young man and woman with different last names lived here, and apparently they both worked. Jack had seen them, even spoken to them occasionally, on Saturdays, when they were home. One of them would meet him at the door or be out in the yard cutting the grass or washing a car. Neither of them appeared to be old enough to receive social security benefits, but it didn't surprise Jack when the first check appeared. It bore the name of a woman with the same last name as the man who lived there, and it began showing up shortly after the guy moved in.

She must be his mother, Jack thought when he first noticed the check, but he never saw the older woman. *I bet she's bedridden or in a nursing home.*

Nothing out of the ordinary; happened all the time.

As Jack approached the house, he thought he saw the door move, just slightly. He fingered through the mail and, sure enough, the check he normally delivered on the 3rd of the month was missing. It had gone to Annandale in the misdirected tray.

Murphy's law: if they're home, I won't have their check, he thought. *I hope this doesn't take long—or get nasty.*

Jack marshaled his people-skills for diplomacy if not mollification. You couldn't screw around with somebody's money and expect them to be okay with it.

He stepped up onto the porch. No one came to the door.

Maybe whoever that was didn't see me coming.

He hoped they hadn't. Maybe he could be gone before they found out the check was missing. It seemed like a coward's way out, but maybe it would save him from the implacable ire sure to arise.

And they can call Morey for an explanation.

Jack harbored a certain satisfaction in thinking that Morey would have to handle the grief.

Forgive your enemies, Jack's mother told him.

I know, I know, he answered, *but it's hard, mom, it's hard.*

Forgive them anyway.

I know.

He flipped open the mailbox that was hanging by the door, dropped the mail in, and let the lid fall shut. Not a lot of noise, but enough so it didn't seem like he was trying to sneak off. He turned to walk away. No one came to the door.

Good, he thought.

Inside the house, someone waited; someone who wanted to get the check and get out of there; someone who didn't want to be seen. Eyes watched like a cat through a sliver of space between the curtains and the front window as Jack rounded the hedge into the neighbor's yard. As soon as Jack was out of sight, the door opened enough for a hand to reach into the mailbox. The hand removed the mail, and the lid dropped with a metal clank. The watcher winced. The arm retreated into the house, and the door closed.

Jack had already gone around the hedge that separated one yard from the next, but he still heard the lid drop and the door close. He winced at about the same time as the person who dropped the lid did. He continued walking, but he listened for the all too familiar sound of a disgruntled patron yelling, 'Hey! Mailman! Wait a minute!' But no one called out. He climbed the steps to the next mailbox and turned to leave. From up here, he could see over the shrubbery. No one came out, so he kept going.

No one came out, but inside the house a voice repeating, *Damn! I need that check!*

The phone rang with startling clarity and shattered the moment. After six rings, the answering machine took a message: "Hi, Honey," the speaker cooed. "Take me to dinner tonight, okay? I'll be home on time. Love you." A small click ended the transmission.

Chapter 5

It was close to noon when Jack finished delivering mail to Hill Street. He drove to a supermarket just off his route and bought a cup of strawberry yogurt, one large oatmeal-raisin cookie and a bottle of water. The cookie would gratify his hypoglycaemic craving for sugar, now that he didn't have all the alcohol that he used to use for fuel. He ate yogurt for protein and drank water out of necessity. Dehydration posed a real threat to people working outside in the Virginia heat wave. Every station on the radio broadcast warnings about working outside, but how else could you deliver mail?

The yogurt, the cookie and the water were all the meal Jack could handle today, knowing he would have to continue working in the heat. When he first started carrying mail, carriers started early in the morning and finished early in the day, usually before lunch. The routes were shorter and people didn't get as much mail.

Back then, too, the carriers sorted all of their own mail. Now, machines sorted most of it, but it had to be checked. Machines didn't know who had moved, or who wanted their mail held while they were away, or who had died, or who had gone off to college. And sometimes couples separated or divorced, and then God help you if you delivered his mail to her or her mail to him. Occasionally people threatened the Postal Service in general or clerks and carriers individually, either with law suits or physical assault, but usually nothing came of it.

The upshot of having machines help sort the mail was that Jack started work later, delivered more mail, and spent more time in the heat. Air quality meant nothing to managers like Morey. When the Virginia

Department of Environmental Quality issued a code red for pollutants, meaning people should "...limit or reschedule strenuous outdoor activity," carriers in Jack's office hit the street with the same amount of mail and the same number of stops as any other day. And they were expected to finish in the same amount of time: no extra breaks; just keep on going.

Jack set his lunch on top of a tray of mail and drove to a spot on the perimeter of the supermarket parking lot where a small tree cast a shadow just large enough to protect him from the direct rays of the sun. It was just a stick with some leaves, but if he didn't move around too much Jack could sit in the shade. He opened the doors on both sides of the truck and sweated anyway as he consumed his meagre rations.

The Postal Service allowed carriers thirty minutes for lunch, but that included driving time. Jack didn't know if Morey had gone back to the air-conditioned office or not, so he didn't want to take any chances by over extending his break. Twenty minutes after starting his lunch, he returned to his route and finished his deliveries.

By the time he was done, three more customers had questioned him about their Social Security checks. He had to refer one of them to Morey. That made two for the day who would be calling and asking for Jack's supervisor. And postal managers like Morey didn't like direct contact with the people they were supposed to be serving, so Jack was counting on a nasty confrontation when he finished his route.

Drenched in sweat and feeling like a hot, dirty sponge, he returned to the post office. His legs felt cramped, and his yogurt and cookie had sunk like the Titanic in the water he had drunk. He backed up to the loading dock, climbed out of his truck and walked to the end of the loading area. He used the steps to get up on the dock, another rule he obeyed just in case Morey was watching.

As he entered the air-conditioned post office and left the soggy, August day outside, he felt a chill through his sweat soaked clothes. With the industrial-strength air conditioning on, it must have been 70° in the building, keeping Morey and the clerks nice and cool while Jack and the rest of the carriers had spent the last several hours in 98° of heat and humidity. One of the clerks walked past with a sweater on.

I think my underwear is going to freeze, he thought. *I wonder if it will shatter when I bend.*

He grabbed a nutting truck, one of those yellow platforms with wheels, a skid or a float as they were sometimes called, and headed back out to the loading dock. But Jack slowed down as he passed behind the post office box section. He tried to look indifferent and cast a furtive glance in that direction hoping to see Julia there. She worked sometimes in the afternoon changing locks on the boxes that had been vacated and were ready to rent again. Jack and Julia had developed a pleasant camaraderie, and Jack always enjoyed seeing her, maybe more than just a friend would. Part of him wished their relationship would develop into something more, but he wasn't pushing it. Good friends were hard to find, and he didn't want to screw up what they already had. Besides, his emotions were still twisted, partly from divorce and partly from his sabbatical from alcohol. His relationship to beer had had a more profound effect on him than almost anything else. In his head he heard Nico and the Velvet Underground divulge their abandonment to heroine:....*it's my wife, it's my life....*

Just like that, he told himself.

He hadn't had a drink in six months, but he wasn't automatically sober, not after a couple of decades of drunkenness.

Maybe I'm not ready for una enamorada, but Julia would be the one, if..., but life was filled with *ifs* and *what ifs* and, in Jack's case, some frustrating *if onlys.*

He didn't see Julia working in the box section, and disappointed, he was about to turn away from the empty work area when someone walked out from behind the row of mail cases that backed up to it. Julia was still working, and she had seen Jack come in. She glanced to her left and then to her right to make sure no one was watching, and then she winked. Little things like that had reached the rumor mill, and she and Jack both tried unsuccessfully to keep the gossips from spreading too many lies. Still, anyone who cared to notice suspected something more than amity between them.

Jack tried to smother a smile that would have outgrown his face, and he ended up with a smirk instead. She had that effect on him.

Like most men, Jack enjoyed being with women, but currently no one special occupied his time or his heart. Since his wife left him three years ago, only Julia had struck him in any kind of personal way. He didn't understand what it was about Julia that had apprehended him. Her hair was not gleaming blue/black, like so many Latinas. It was not primped, poofed, permed, curled or colored. Sometimes it wasn't even combed. Make-up rarely marred her features, which were a combination of her mother's Spanish descent from seafaring explorers and a hint of her father's native Inca roots from the other side of the Andes, near the Amazon River. Her attire usually resembled her hair: occasionally disheveled, but she smelled clean, and looked healthy and attractive. Besides, she was smart, funny and kind. And kindness was a rarity these days, especially among the ranks of postal employees, whether they were workers or managers.

Jack wheeled the nutting truck out through the impact doors to the loading dock, wishing he could stop and talk to Julia, but he thought he'd better not, at least not yet. He took the empty trays out of his truck and drove the hollow vehicle to the back of the parking lot. He parked it in its assigned parking space and locked the doors, and then, as he turned to go inside, he bumped into Julia. She was standing right in front of him, just the two of them, trapped in the eighteen inches between parked mail trucks. He hadn't seen her follow him out.

"Julia!" he exclaimed, happy and more than a little surprised. "What are you doing here so late?" he asked.

It was a stupid question. He knew Julia worked late often, but he had to say something. Being so close to her always caused an internal upheaval in Jack and his mental agility suffered instantly.

Julia smiled, and the last of Jack's acuity evaporated.

"Maybe if you don't run over me I will tell you," she said. Then she laughed and, so Jack wouldn't feel anymore foolish than he already did, she added, "I worked overtime today. I need some money."

She spoke with an accent that Jack found alluring. Her native tongue was so much softer than his.

But why did she come out here? he wondered.

Now, standing close to each other in between the parked mail trucks, he hoped her motives were amorously driven, but somehow he doubted it.

"So what are you going to buy with all this money?" Jack asked.

"I just need to pay my bills, Jack, you know that," she said coyly. "But I thought you should know there was a lot of talking about you today. Morey and one of those new guys, you know, the *tranees*, I think are going to stab your back."

The *tranees* were really the "trainees," but Jack enjoyed their new Span/ingles title. He liked it enough that, despite the news of a plot for his destruction, he laughed. His heart rate increased, but anticipation of the looming confrontation with Morey had nothing to do with it. Julia's immediacy sent a current of electricity through him, and everything else paled in comparison.

"I know," Jack replied through his grin. "I gave his phone number to a couple of disgruntled postal patrons. He probably wants to fire me. But thanks for the warning." He continued to smile.

"De nada," she said as she winked again, "y cuidate."

Julia knew that Jack could speak a few words of Spanish, words and phrases he had picked up in the work place, and she took every opportunity to encourage him to learn more. Sometimes she jokingly insisted that he master her language if they were to converse, because she would certainly never master his. He had to admit that English had as many exceptions as rules.

"But you're an exceptional person," he had once told her, and he meant for it to sound like a joke, only he wasn't joking.

Julia turned and walked back to the building. Jack watched her walk and felt something between elation and collapse.

Is it just the heat? Or maybe I didn't have enough for lunch. Yeah, low blood sugar, that's it, he told himself, but he knew that wasn't it at all.

Jack stood there for a moment, grinning. He watched her go inside. She looked so wholesome, a stark contrast to her surroundings. He let a moment lapse and followed her into the building. There was no sense in feeding the rumor mill by walking in together.

♠

Julia was already back at work changing locks in the box section. When she heard the impact doors swing open and then close again, she risked a glance in their direction, and it was Jack's turn to wink. She held her lips tightly together to keep from smiling, but one corner of her mouth turned up anyway.

Jack hauled the empty trays and tubs back to his case, one cubicle among many, and Morey approached with a supervisor/trainee in tow.

"I want to see you in my office after you clear the cage," Morey said, his voice professionally cold and loud enough for anyone around to hear.

"Sure," Jack answered Morey as if he didn't have a clue why the supervisor would want to see him.

'Clearing the cage' meant Jack had to hand over any money he had collected, whether for postage due, customs due or COD items. He also had keys, both for his truck and for mail collection boxes, apartment buildings and cluster boxes. And he had receipts for certified, registered and insured mail. He had signed for everything that morning, and now he had to clear his name for each item.

The cage literally was a cage, with chain link sides and top and a locking, wire mesh door. It was meant to keep people out, but sometimes it looked more like a cell to keep a clerk in. Many of the employees felt trapped anyway, so the cage appeared to belong in the office and the clerk inside usually felt protected from the other prisoners as opposed to one of the imprisoned.

The cage clerk, usually friendly, distanced herself from Jack today.

Self preservation, Jack thought. *She knows I'm in trouble.* He didn't hold it against her.

He finished up at the cage and ambled toward Morey's office, collecting sideways glances from a few co-workers. He shook off a claustrophobic feeling, like he was running a gauntlet where his peers all threw funny looks at him. Everybody knew nothing good would come of the confrontation, but they all wanted to watch. Morbidity hung in the air.

Judging by the vibes, Jack figured he was in a lot of trouble.

Over a couple of phone calls, he thought. *Or he's still pissed off about this morning.*

He walked into Morey's office. A management trainee sat in chair beside Morey's desk.

"Close the door and sit," Morey ordered and Jack did.

Actually, he sprawled, and it felt good after carrying mail for miles in the excessive heat.

Jack was entitled to a witness, a union representative, but he didn't ask for one. He knew that, despite any character references from the rabble outside the office, he would not be winning any medals today, so he just did as he was told, foregoing the formality of another body in the room.

"I have a witness here to your insolence and insubordination, Mr. Casey," Morey said, indicating his protégé sitting next to his desk. "He was in my car when I found you on your route today."

"Really?" Jack hid his surprise and looked directly at the other man in the room. "And where was that?" Jack asked, without averting his eyes.

The trainee looked worried and glanced at his boss.

"You know damned well where it was," Morey yelled.

"I wasn't talking to you," Jack said without hesitation. "I was talking to the guy who was in your car. Where was that?"

He continued staring at the other man, who still couldn't meet his gaze. Jack knew the guy hadn't been there. Morey's car had been empty. The 'tranee,' as Julia would have called him, was being used, a liar in training.

"I'm suspending you for two weeks without pay effective immediately!" Morey leveled his verbal assault at Jack. "You were unsafe in your vehicle, and you were insubordinate!"

"Don't I get a formal reprimand or a letter of warning or something for a first offense? Doesn't that come before a suspension without pay?" Jack remained calm. He knew the rules, but he knew he was getting the suspension, anyway. He just didn't want to cave in right away. Besides, the fun in the life lay in teasing Morey, like a cat playing with its food.

"You've had all the warnings you're going to get! You've been nothing but trouble since I came here!" Morey was red and purple and close to a tootsie roll pop in appearance.

"No, I think it was a couple of months *after* you came here. It took me awhile to figure out what a dishonest creep you are."

Jack got up and walked out before Morey could find his tongue. He slammed the door behind him, but his face belied any anger. In fact, he had some difficulty containing himself. It wasn't often that he was able to win two verbal skirmishes with Morey in one day. Of course, Morey won the war by default. It came with his title. But, still, despite two weeks without pay, Jack felt good.

"Hey Jack, did you get a good review?" someone asked from behind a row of route cases.

A few laughs went up, but they were tentative, like the first early-evening bursts on the Fourth of July. Nobody wanted to attract any attention that might put him or her on Morey's bad side and incur punitive damages. With Morey, one never knew.

"No, I don't think he likes the way I drive."

"Then tell him to get off the sidewalk," added a familiar disembodied voice.

"That's old, Larry, like you," Jack replied.

Jack headed toward the door, but he looked to see if Julia was still around. He noticed her across the workroom floor, about eighty feet away. He wanted to say 'good-bye' or 'see you later' or something before he left for two weeks, but he didn't want to yell. He felt like enough of a spectacle already. He headed over to where she was working. She hadn't seen him.

"Hey Julia," he said to get her attention.

She turned away from what she was doing, happy to see him but concerned.

"What happened?" she asked. "It sounds awfully loud in the office!"

"Oh, Morey gave me a two-week vacation," Jack offered.

"Oh rreeeally?" she mocked. "He must like you a lot."

"Not rreeeally," Jack said. "I don't think he likes me at all."

They laughed, and it brought about an instant unification of spirit.

After a moment, Julia said, "I'm finished here. Are you leaving now?" She had been stretching her workday a little, just to see what would happen to Jack.

"Oh yeah," Jack replied. "I'm finished here."

Julia gathered her apron, gloves and lunch container and they walked out the back door to the employees parking area. Jack felt a foolish desire to hold her hand and glanced at Julia to see if she felt the same way, as if he could tell by looking. She glanced back at him, smiling. Jack's aches and pains disappeared.

Outside, they moved to the left of the door. Neither wanted to say good-bye, but neither of them said so. Wordlessly, they stopped walking at the edge of the parking lot. Jack thought about suggesting they get a cup of coffee, maybe on the weekend or even right now. The idea of spending an entire afternoon and evening with Julia appealed to him.

"What are you going to do on your vacation?" Julia asked.

"Not much," Jack said. "It doesn't include any money."

The banter continued and Jack waited patiently for the right place in their conversation to mention seeing each other outside of the post office. It would be something new for them. As they spoke, they started finding reasons to touch; there was a friendly bump or a hand placed gently on an arm. From a distance they appeared to be dancing toward a more intimate communion.

Before Jack could summon the courage to broach the subject of coffee together, the rumble of a finely tuned power plant, circa 1969, shattered the mood. A lime-green Camaro, fuzzy dice swinging from the rear-view mirror, seemed to growl as it approached. Everyone within ear-shot looked at the car.

Jack and Julia looked, too, and then turned back to each other.

Julia said, "I need to go, Jack. That's my ride."

Jack looked back to the lime-green machine, and his eyes locked onto the eyes of a muscled Latino in a tank top. The skin-tight haircut made it difficult to tell if he was military or a gang banger, but, either way, he wasn't her father, and he wasn't smiling.

Jack looked back at Julia.

"Keep in touch, okay?" she said sheepishly.

Her eyes imparted a reluctance to leave, but she had to go.

"Yeah, sure, take it easy," Jack said, and his voice belied the sinking feeling in his gut.

He watched Julia walk to the car and get in. She waved one more time as the driver glared at him, and then she and her 'ride' drove away.

Chapter 6

Angel picked up Julia from the post office and made sure she was safely in their apartment before he headed for work himself.

As he drove, he wondered, *Who was that guy she was talking to?*

He had asked her when he picked her up, but she shrugged and said it was just some guy she worked with. He worried about her. She was a big girl and he trusted her, but she could be impulsive. Angel cared about her more than he did about anything else in the world. He would keep her on his radar. He would keep that guy she worked with on his radar, too.

Jack was still standing by the Post Office and wishing Julia hadn't left, when Morey's voice came over the outside PA speaker. It sounded like a lunatic used car salesman.

"Jack Casey," the voice raged, "Report to the supervisor's office, NOW."

Jack carried his preoccupation with Julia back into the building and then to the office where Morey stood, flapping a handful of checks at him.

"I've got customers complaining. They want their checks and you're going to deliver them."

Five minutes earlier, Morey had hung up the phone and gone to the distribution case, where he pulled out some of the next day's letter mail for Jack's route, mail that had arrived after the carriers hit the street that morning. The social security checks from Annandale were all there and easy to spot by the orange/brown, check-sized US Treasury envelopes.

"Get these delivered now, Casey!"

"Sure, Morey," Jack said. "Are we all going back out on overtime today, or just me? I thought I was suspended without pay?"

"Don't give me any of your crap, and don't even think about filing a grievance," Morey answered. "It's *your* customers who seem to feel the need to complain in order to get any service."

Jack smiled. Morey reminded him of Louie in Taxi.

Who complained?" Jack asked, raising his eyebrows and knowing he wouldn't get an answer.

"Just deliver the checks, Casey," Morey ordered.

In fact, Morey didn't know who had complained, only that the phone call frightened him. The voice wasn't screaming in uncontrolled anger. The caller sounded calm and hard, like someone who got his way or put someone else through hell.

"I want that check now," the voice commanded.

Malevolence seemed to pass through the wire. It wasn't the voice of an older man, like an over 65 retiree waiting for a social security check. Morey felt a shiver go right through him.

"What's your address, sir," Morey had replied. "I'll see if I can find it and get it to you this afternoon."

He hated backing down, but fear was a great motivator.

"You goddamn well better find it," the voice said, "or I'll come get it from you."

The caller's volume remained in the normal range, but the voice was cold and soulless and hard as granite, and Morey's heart thumped against his chest like depth charges shaking an underwater world. His abdominal cavity felt empty.

"I live on Maple Street."

The line went dead.

Anxiety gripped the caller as he hung up the phone. He didn't want anyone to know where he was. He needed time. Unfortunately, he also needed that check from the post office, so he had called. Now he had no way of knowing whether the check would show up. He was reasonably sure he had scared the idiot on the phone, but that still didn't mean the bureaucrat would find the check and get it to him.

And there was the stolen truck he needed to ditch. Cops would be looking for it by tonight or tomorrow. He certainly didn't want them to find it anywhere near here.

"*Sh.t!*" The word escaped like a whispered hiss.

He left the house the way he had come, through the back door. He left everything the way he had found it and returned to the pick up truck he had parked one street over. He wheeled down the street and around the block and parked at the end of Maple Street. There was a car dealership at the corner where Maple intersected the fast food strip in Fairfax. He hoped he looked like a mechanic on lunch break to anyone who might notice him. He decided to sit and wait where he could see the bungalow.

Now, he thought, *How long should I wait for the goddamn mailman? No more than an hour*, he told himself. *Then I'm outta here. I'll find some other way to survive a few days.*

He waited long enough to begin doubting himself and began trying to justify his actions. He was only taking what was his. Devoid of a healthy conscience, he remained oblivious to the fundamental evil of his aberrant behavior.

Where is that worthless f...of a mailman with the check?

At that moment, as if looking for a beating, Jack rounded the corner at the far end of the street. The watcher stopped breathing, stopped thinking, and swallowed hard. The mail truck came to a halt a half a block short of the bungalow.

He'll stop again, he thought. *C'mon, you bastard*, he muttered.

He stared as Jack leapt from the 'wrong' side of the odd truck and took the four steps up from the sidewalk two at a time. He reached the old porch and dropped something in the mailbox, turning as he did to walk briskly across the street and do the same at that house. He trotted back to the truck and was turning the key before his butt hit the seat. He passed by four houses and then repeated the process at a fifth. Walking door to door may have been just as efficient.

The man watching Jack could see the brown envelopes that he left in each mailbox. He knew they were Social Security checks, and his heart beat faster in anticipation. He would cash the check to tide him over. His confidence grew. He approached euphoria and fought to control it. He needed to keep his focus if he wanted to remain free for the next few days.

The mail truck moved up the street and stopped in front of the bungalow. Jack delivered a check to the house on his right. The man didn't breathe while Jack crossed the street and delivered a check with Lucille Hardin's name on it.

Now get the hell out of here, he murmured at the windshield, watching Jack return to the truck.

Jack hopped back into the delivery vehicle and drove to the end of Maple Street, heading straight toward the auto body shop. He saw the man in the pick-up sitting in the shade on his left.

A mechanic taking a break, his subconscious said, though the man seemed fidgety and irritated. A scowl blemished his face, and he cast a glance that both sought and avoided eye contact. He looked away as Jack passed. He also looked familiar.

I must have seen him here before, Jack thought, as his mind looked for a way to make sense of the familiarity.

The man in the truck calmed himself for a moment, thinking that all had gone well. But his heart started pounding again, knowing that he had to return to the house to get the check.

The less I'm seen the better, but I gotta get that check now

He turned the key in the ignition and drove straight up the street without so much as pulling away from the curb. He stopped in front of the bungalow, not in the driveway.

Stay calm, gotta stay calm, he chanted. *Anyway, it's my check.*

He left the motor running and walked up to the front door. He paused, opening the mailbox. The brown envelope was there, and he slipped it into his shirt pocket. To any outside observer, he could have been whistling the theme to "The Andy Griffith Show" on his way back to the truck.

Across the street, there was an outside observer: Ethel Bergen watched from her window. Jack's not-so-light footsteps on her porch earlier had brought her to the front of her house. Her anger subsided when she found her overdue-check, and after retrieving her mail for the second time that day, she noticed the truck stopped in front of the bungalow.

Seeing the distinctive brown envelope protruding from the man's pocket, she thought, *No one in that house is old enough to receive a social security check! I wonder if this is one of those fraud scams going on.*

She went to her phone and dialed the number she had written on the pad of paper beside it. Once you got the Social Security Office's phone number, you kept it. God only knew how many times she had had to call before. Any time her check didn't arrive by one o'clock so she called. The people she spoke to tried to tell her that the time of delivery wasn't guaranteed, but she knew better.

I'll use the drive-thru and be less conspicuous. That little bitch in there won't know my height or weight, or what I'm wearing. Probably won't even notice what color the truck is, and I'll be rid of it soon enough, anyway.

He stopped at the end of the line to the window farthest from the teller, the line that had to use the pneumatic tube. He didn't want to get any closer than necessary. He waited behind a blue BMW. A yellow, convertible VW 'beetle' carrying two 'look-at-me,' office workers stood in front of the 'beemer.' They would certainly be more memorable than a blue collar worker in a pick-up truck. He waited impatiently as he listened to the garble of the intercom and the contrasting, clear answers:

"Yes, this is two transactions. I want to deposit the check and...*blah blah blah...*"

He willed them to move, vitriol pouring out his window. After too many minutes, they finished. The business man in the 'beemer' knew what he wanted to do and had his paperwork ready by the time he pulled up to the window. He finished quickly and pulled away.

...*about damn time*, he thought, and drove to the column with the pneumatic tube system.

"Good afternoon," crackled the intercom, and he saw a girl who looked too young to be handling money leaning toward a microphone. "How may I help you...?"

After what seemed an eternity, he pulled away with $742.

...*about damn time*, he raged to himself again.

He headed out of Fairfax, west on Route 29.

Chapter 7

Jack returned to the post office. This time there was no wink from Julia. She was long gone with the caballero and his muscle car. On a brighter note, there was no Morey. He certainly wouldn't bother hanging around to make sure Jack's checks got delivered, even though he should have. After all, he did send Jack back out.

I'm outta here, too, Jack thought.

He turned in his truck keys for the second time and left the mostly empty building.

He was thinking, *Two weeks off; nice, but I have a feeling my credit card is going to suffer.*

Jack didn't have a lot of money saved. He had just managed to keep things together, just enough to buy out his ex's share of their rambler.

He hit the ignition on his '71 Chevrolet and it roared to life. It didn't look like much, but Jack kept it running right. The Chevy 350ci engine exemplified the decline of the muscle car era, but at least it was hitting on all eight cylinders. He pulled away from the Post Office parking lot, and headed toward his empty, brick rambler in Sterling, VA. The house was his daily reminder of an equally abandoned marriage.

He felt drained when he arrived; it had been a long day and a hot one. He traipsed into the kitchen from the garage, and the Bug met him at the door.

"The house isn't completely empty, is it, Bug?"

The wiry mutt stretched and yawned and said something like 'ohhoow.' His tail wagged, and he looked toward the sliding glass door by the table and then back at Jack.

"I know," Jack said. "You need out, don't you?"

Jack had cared for his mother, Eileen, everyday for months before she succumbed to the cancer that killed her, and the Bug, too, had depended on Jack for his daily needs while Eileen's body deteriorated. She had adopted the ugly little beast four years earlier when he wandered into her yard looking dirty and hungry. She fed him and cleaned him and kept him. She called him Chauncy, but Jack called him the Bug and told his mother he still looked dirty and hungry four years later. They both loved the little guy and after the funeral, orphaned for the second time, the Bug went home with Jack.

Out in the back yard, Bug did what he needed to do and wanted back in. He wanted to be with Jack, and to eat, not necessarily in that order. Jack had already put dry dog food and water out, and he was talking to a Pizza Haven guy while he slid open the door for Bug.

"Yeah, with mushrooms," he said and slid the door shut.

He bent down and scratched Bug's ears, an act of kindness received with an exuberance known only to dogs.

"Yeah, for delivery," Jack said.

He finished with the order and hung up.

"This should be good for a couple of meals, huh, Bug? Dinner and breakfast."

Wolfing down his own meal, Bug ignored Jack who was trying to justify spending twelve bucks when he was temporarily unemployed. He knew he was kidding himself. He was just too tired to fix anything. Besides, there wasn't anything to fix. Other than dog food, Jack didn't keep much in the pantry.

Jack grabbed the remote for his sound system and manipulated the CD changer until he heard Springsteen singing *Radio Nowhere*.

"Is there anybody alive out there?" he mumbled as he headed for the shower with the Bug at his side.

He adjusted the water, not too hot for the dog because:

"Surprise," he said and laughed as he grabbed the unsuspecting, little guy before he could get away. "Yeah, you too. At least once a month, whether you need it or not, you little stinker."

Jack and the hairy little dude would be clean, for a while, anyway.

We'll be all right, mom.
I know, Jackie, I know.

The troubled man reached Interstate 66 two miles ahead of Angel, and he pulled the pick-up into a rest area. He needed the bathroom and he was tired and hungry. Larceny was hard work.

First the bathroom, then the vending machines will have to do for dinner.

He felt relatively safe, but he didn't want anyone to notice him.

There were a couple of guys in the bathroom who probably belonged to one or two of a half dozen big rigs parked in long spaces out front. He avoided eye contact with them. He didn't speak, and neither did they. Once outside the bathroom, he approached the vending machines and examined the unsavory food choices through a glass panel. Suddenly, the reflection of a large, gray sedan appeared. He glanced back and saw a Virginia State Trooper, still in the cruiser, putting on his hat.

Jesus, he thought. *I don't need this cowboy now.*

He slid his hand past the $742 in his pocket and produced some change. He dropped some in the machine, and checked the reflection of the cruiser again: the empty cruiser.

Shit, shit, shit, shit, shit! He muttered as he punched C 10, and watched the Oreos drop.

"Is there a problem, sir?"

The voice came from behind him, and he nearly needed the bathroom again.

"Uh, no, uh, just hit the wrong button," he managed without turning more than a quarter turn. "But these will do," he added, trying to sound normal.

"All right then, sir, have a good evening," Angel Iglesias replied, and dropped some coins into the coffee machine.

Angel was on his right, so he turned to his left and walked back to the stolen pick-up. He got in without slamming the door. The trooper still had his back to the parking lot when the old GMC truck started.

The driver was thinking, *Don't turn around, don't turn around, don't turn around,* and simultaneously, *are the tags expired? Are the right stickers on the windshield?*

He eased out of the parking place and started moving toward the interstate. He looked in the rearview mirror more than the road. Angel turned with coffee in hand and seemed to watch him, then walked back to his cruiser.

Gotta get outta here!

His emotions reeled as he hit the interstate and ran the old truck up to 70 mph. He was at the next exit in less than five minutes and he went east on some county road to nowhere. No one followed. His stomach churned, but not from hunger.

Angel sipped a little coffee before firing up the power packed State Police cruiser. He pulled out of the rest area and accelerated. Almost immediately, he heard what sounded like a shot from a large caliber weapon. He froze and then nearly ducked, but he forced himself to look around. A truck up ahead began to wag its trailer, and the separated tread from a huge recap flew over two cars and landed in the right lane of the busy highway. Two cars swerved to avoid the obstacle before Angel reached it.

He pulled to the side of the highway as he lit the blue strobes on the roof and the lights in the rear window and in the grill. Angel hated being on the side of an interstate highway. People drove too fast and paid too little attention, and now they would be startled by the big, black tire tread curled and twisted in their path. The highway was dangerous enough without that thing blocking a lane.

He popped his trunk and lit a flare and started walking back in the direction of the tread. The light traffic slowed and most drivers changed lanes; it was the law. When he thought it was safe Angel walked to the spent rubber and dragged it to the side of the road. It was warm, almost hot. He had to be careful with the braided steel protruding from the sides of the rubber. They were as sharp as needles.

The anxious thief drove the pick up on back roads until he came to a house sitting alone in the dust of a dirt road. He would hide the truck here and take the old car that sat, backed into the wooden garage beside the house. He grabbed the pistol on the seat beside him and pushed it into his waistband as he climbed out of the truck. He walked up to the house, turned the doorknob and walked in.

When he waved off the flies and smelled and saw the rotting corpse he was furious. He had nursed a love/hate relationship with his mother, as if it were the most precious of all bonds. And it had been precious, in the repulsive, vomity way of Tolkien's Smeegle. His fury stemmed partly from his mother's death, but mostly from someone other than him killing her. If anyone had the right to kill her, he did. Those things she made him do, gave him the right.

He changed his plans. Someone would pay for this, and he knew who.

He had to jump-start the old car with cables from the toolbox in the truck. He pulled the car out and put the truck in the shed. He closed the doors, and then took off. He drove right past Esther Aubrey's house, the old bitch that used to think she was caring for him; but instead of getting as far away as he could get from Northern Virginia, he headed back to Fairfax. He had unfinished business there.

It was only minutes after Race pulled away that Esther Aubrey called the Virginia State Police. Angel Iglesias got the call from Rita at dispatch about a possible stolen car and exited I-66, headed for Thelma Hardin's house.

Chapter 8

Angel thanked God he was off the interstate as he drove to the Hardin residence. He wasn't nearly so thankful when he found Mrs. Hardin sitting in a rocker in the living room just inside the unlatched front door. After backing away from the cloud of flies, he had vomited and then called in. He described the situation and waited for the Virginia State Police homicide investigators, but the first officials on the scene were from the County Sheriff's Department, two men in one car. The driver was, in fact, the County Sheriff. He wore the brown and tan dress code of a sheriff, a blazer, slacks and a tie. The man next to him wore a blue coat and a red tie on a body reminiscent of a hippo in a tutu. Angel watched them struggle from the car, a large, but not large enough for a hippo, sedan.

"I'm the DA in this county, and this is Sheriff Reisner. We monitored your call," the large man with the red tie said. "We'll take it from here, trooper."

Angel looked at them as they approached. Dust rose in little clouds around their shoes. The Sheriff stopped in front of Angel and started to offer his hand, but he stopped when Angel grabbed the DA's arm. The DA had continued walking past Angel toward the house.

"What the…"

"Sir, you can't go in there," Angel said. "Forensics goes in first."

"I believe I told you we would take it from here," steamed the big man.

"No, sir," Angel replied without releasing his grip or his gaze. "Forensics goes in first."

Angel knew the modus operandi for the Commonwealth of Virginia and the State Police, and he would not be moved.

"Sheriff, get this man off me, or I will!"

"Calm down, Don. We can have our own forensics check it out. It's still our case," said Sheriff Reisner.

He put his hand on Don Cambridge's shoulder but without applying much pressure. Angel, on the other hand, still had a firm grip on the man's arm, and he had no intention of letting go unless the man stepped back. After a moment electrified by the clash, Don Cambridge stepped back.

"Make no mistake, trooper, this is my case. You may go now."

Angel looked directly into the DA's face, but he said nothing and he did not move.

"Don, we need to question the trooper. He found the body, you know, first on the scene and all."

"I can get back to…" he paused and looked at Angel's name tag, "Trooper Igglissyaz. Why don't you go ahead and call our investigative team."

"My name is Trooper Iglesias. I believe the State Homicide Investigators are on the way, sir," Angel said.

His demeanor remained professional, almost military. The temperature seemed to drop to zero Kelvin as all molecular activity froze.

"You listen to me you little…"

"Don! Take it easy!" Sheriff Reisner could have been talking to a stump with a tie.

Don spun to face Angel head-on, and Angel, instead of backing up, moved forward. Their faces were less than three inches apart, and the façade of civility nearly shattered. Sheriff Reisner was reaching between them as tires crunched the rocks at the head of the short, dirt driveway. The three heads turned and the scene froze.

Inside the car, Detective John Hammond said, "Looks like Trooper Iglesias is making friends again."

"He's good at that," Detective Reilly snickered and looked down to cover his grin as he shut off the engine of the unmarked, state vehicle. There wasn't any point in throwing gasoline on a fire.

Both state investigators were in their late forties and had spent time in Angel's shoes. They were glad to be out of his shoes now and had to laugh at some of the situations they no longer dealt with. They knew they were in charge of this investigation, whether the county sheriff and DA knew it or not. Neither Hammond nor Reilly hesitated getting out of the car.

"Trooper Iglesias," Reilly said like some happy Irishman walking between the glut of cruisers toward Angel.

John Hammond followed his partner, towering over the rest of the men.

"Yes, sir," said Angel, still looking back at the DA and not moving.

Reilly wanted desperately to ask Angel if he and the rotund man in front of him were going to dance, but he refrained. Still, his mirth lurked just under the surface. John Reilly, everyone called him Reilly in deference to John Hammond, kept a sense of humor despite his job and its ugly view of life and death. Now he addressed the Sheriff and the DA, certain that they knew their place in the chain of command:

"Gentlemen, if you'll excuse us, we'll keep you apprised of our progress."

"Now just a minute here…"

"I'm going to need some ID, sir," John Hammond interjected, "or I'll have to ask you to leave the scene." John could give lessons in intimidation.

"I'm the DA here and I'll let…"

Reilly jumped back into the conversation: "You can stay here, then, but we'll need you stay out of the way for now."

He had the DA's head ratcheting between him and Hammond like a spectator at Wimbledon.

Sheriff Reisner, a good judge of people and situations, assumed a relaxed, even submissive attitude.

Don Cambridge, the DA, who normally bullied his foes, felt like a chew toy between two pit bulls. He was outnumbered and outclassed. He stepped back toward Sheriff Reisner followed by three pairs of Virginia State Police eyes.

"I expect to be a part of this investigation," he blustered.

The three State law-enforcement officers looked at him until he looked away.

They had work to do.

Chapter 9

Sandi left the airport, glad to be going home. The day had dragged, but now it was over.

"God, what I wouldn't do to get out of working for the rest of my life!"

She battled the rush hour traffic on Route 28 heading from Dulles IAD toward Route 50. She took a right hand exit to go east on Route 50, toward Fairfax and against Virginia's influx of traffic returning from downtown DC, but the traffic on her side of the highway was a mess, too.

It hadn't always been this way. She remembered going places with her parents ages ago and not waiting: not at traffic signals; not for other cars; not speeding up and slowing down, but it seemed to be this way most of the time now.

Fortunately she had air conditioning and a CD player in her Porsche. Still she mantained her acrimonious attitude. She felt sticky and greasy at the same time, that feeling that seems to creep up between showers. She wanted to wash her face, her feet, and her hair. She wanted to wash everywhere. It would feel so good to be clean again…AND go out to dinner.

"I hope Race got my message."

Thirty minutes later, after what should have been a twenty minute drive, she swung into the driveway of the bungalow and climbed out of the sports car. It was expensive, but not really that comfortable.

She walked toward the unlit house and wondered why the lights weren't on. The house seemed empty.

"Is he even home?" She questioned.

Race wandered the back roads in the general direction of Fairfax County. The sun had set, and the moon and stars had a difficult time penetrating the thick Virginia woods. The sparse light Race saw came from occasional spotlights on phone poles in farmyards, mostly quite a bit off the road. The only road markers were little white signs with small black numbers: 795, 608, 797. They were all insignificant backwoods roads winding their way to somewhere.

His paranoia had subsided, or at least retreated a little. Now he was beyond exhaustion, but there was nowhere to sleep. All he could see were ditches, trees, and some homemade mailbox posts wearing their mailboxes like damaged hats. He couldn't pull over anywhere. He would be half on the road and half off—a sure thing for a deputy sheriff to check out, if one happened by.

"Gotta keep goin'," Race thought. "Can't ask for directions in the middle of the night. People will remember something like that."

He drove, never turning unless he had to. Eventually he came to Route 340.

"Alright!" he thought, "Route 340. That runs all the way back to Bentonville and Front Royal."

He hung a left and headed toward more familiar territory. After ten miles he came to a motel near a little town called Grottoes. It was just a little mom and pop kind of motel, and he hoped they would just give him a room and forget he had ever been there. But he knew they wouldn't. There weren't any other cars in the lot. How could they forget the only customer they had that night. Still, he had to sleep, sleep and take care of things in the morning.

He parked in front and thanked a god he didn't believe in that someone was in the office and awake. The young woman seemed disinterested, but wanted to see his ID. He didn't want to give it to her, but he couldn't think of a way out of it. She filled out a short form, filed it, and handed him a key.

"Its room 2, second one down. It has a new mattress. The other one got burned." She seemed to look at him for the first time.

"Thanks," he muttered and left as quickly as possible.

"Good," he thought, and headed toward a bed.

Race had never shown up at home, and Sandi's anticipation of dining out had burned to embers. She fixed a grilled cheese sandwich. That and a bowl of cream of tomato soup with crumbled saltines in it became dinner. The television bored her, and the clock chimed ten.

"Where the hell is he?" she wondered.

She worried. She picked up the phone and dialed.

"Ellen? Hi, this is Sandi. I'm sorry to call so late, but Race isn't home yet, and I wondered if maybe George knew where he had gone."

The voice on the other end sounded mature and calm, but with an undercurrent of anxiety.

"George isn't home either, Sandi. I've been waiting for a call."

"Oh, you're kidding! That's not like him, is it?"

"No," Ellen replied, "but there must be a good explanation."

"Or excuse!" Sandi said, but amended her thoughts. "I'm thinking of Race, of course, not George. He's always so sweet."

"He has his moments," Ellen replied. "I don't know what to think right now. What should we do?"

"Do you think Eddie's wife might know where they are?" Sandi asked.

"Probably not," said Ellen. "I have a feeling that Eddie not showing up immediately after work is not unusual. I suppose every family has its own way of doing things."

"I guess you're right," Sandi said. She had seen Eddie drunk often enough to reconize it as his normal state. "He's a nice little man to see once in a while, but being married to someone who drinks all the time must be hard. Race says he's an alcoholic."

"I suppose," Ellen replied. "I just hate this waiting and not knowing."

"Well, let me know if you hear anything, and I'll do the same. I don't think I'll be sleeping very soundly anyway, so call as soon as you know something," Sandi said.

"Do the same, okay?" said Ellen.

"Sure. Talk to you later."

They hung up.

"It's getting late. Damn him! I don't need to start the week like this!"

Sandi went to bed at eleven. She looked at the clock at twelve. The phone rang at one-seventeen.

"I'm so sorry to bother you," Ellen said.

Her voice wasn't nearly as calm as it had been.

"George still isn't home and hasn't called. I'm worried sick. I wondered if you had heard anything. Is Race there?"

"No," Sandi said. "I'm kind of worried myself."

"I'm going to call the hospitals and...and the police." Ellen's tears were near.

"Why don't I call Prince William hospital to see if they ended up going in that direction? Then I'll call Fair Oaks. You call Fairfax Hospital. I don't think we need to call the police yet."

Sandi knew the older woman didn't want to think anything bad had happened. Ellen didn't want to call the hospitals, much less the police.

"All right," Ellen said. "I'll call you right back, if that's okay."

"Sure," Sandi said. "Talk to you in a few minutes. I'm sure they're okay," she added.

"Okay," Ellen said, and put down the receiver.

"Poor thing," Sandi thought, and then "Where the hell are they?"

She rubbed the sleep from her eyes and went to the kitchen for the phone book.

Chapter 10

At 4:00 A.M. Angel gazed out the window of the apartment he shared with his sister. Julia slept soundly in her room, but Angel was wired. The adrenaline rush of yesterday evening, the body, the sheriff, the DA— Ay Gringo loco. Then he had to go over and over what little information he had with John and Reilly. Nearly two hours later, people from forensics showed up, and he had to show them where he had walked, what he had touched, even where he had puked. Hours passed before he pulled in at the State Police sub-station on Route 50, and drank two cups of coffee while he did the paperwork necessary to complete his shift.

When he got home about three-thirty, he put on more coffee, and now he sat at the window waiting for the sun to come up and thinking. He couldn't stop thinking.

She could have just died right there in the rocker, heart attack or something, he told himself.

But why didn't anyone know? She'd been there long enough to start decomposing. Why didn't anyone come around or call? Why wasn't anyone missing her? Why wasn't anyone suspicious?

"Hi, Baby."

Angel jumped, even before Julia put her arms around him from behind and hugged him and kissed the top of his head.

"Ay, Julia, if I didn't love you I would kill you. You scared me half to death," Angel rattled off in Spanish.

Julia smiled; her eyes closed, and she replied in Spanish, "You wouldn't kill me, Angel. Who would do your laundry?"

Angel held her arms around him for a moment. He loved Julia as a brother should love a sister, never realizing how unusual that was.

"Why aren't you sleeping?" Julia asked and moved toward the coffeemaker.

"Why aren't you?" Angel replied.

"I have to go to work, Angel, and you have to take me. Remember? My car is still in the shop. And why are you still wearing your uniform? When did you get home?" And then, startled, she asked, "My God, Angel, what happened?"

Julia spun to face him with the sudden realization that something terrible could have happened to her brother, her only family.

"Paperwork, little sister. I found a body yesterday. *Una vieja.* Her death is being investigated." He looked at her, saw her worry and added, "I'm okay. Nothing happened."

"Ugh! Your job is gross, Angel."

Julia sorted mail in the box section of the Chantilly Post Office. Because of the light volume, she worked alone, a situation she preferred. Quiet time at the post office eluded most employees; she considered herself fortunate.

Around 7:45 A.M., she caught herself glancing toward the back door where the time clock captured everyone's movements: starting, stopping, out-to-lunch, in-from-lunch, changing activities, and the carriers recorded their leaving and returning times. Some of the early carriers were walking in, glancing at the time, and going to their lockers or to get a cup of coffee before starting their day.

Ay, Dios, Julia thought, *I'm looking for Jack, and he won't be here!*

Her own preoccupation with Jack caused her to wonder. Suddenly her day became just another day with nothing special to look forward to.

Quiero un hombre blanco como Jack? Am I wanting a man so white as Jack? she asked herself, and smiled.

Julia continued her work, but without much enthusiasm. She missed the days when she knew Jack was in the building, and she missed wondering if he would speak to her, and if maybe they would accidentally meet in the break room. Lately, though, their encounters occurred more by design than chance. Sometimes she waited for Jack to take his morning break, and then she took hers. She noticed, too, that Jack found reasons to walk by her work area, she thought just to see her.

Espero, I hope so, she told herself, and smiled.

Tuesday dawned, and became for Jack, day one of an unpaid vacation. He slept until eight o'clock, late for him. When he woke up he felt pretty good. He had the day to himself.

In the kitchen of his small house, he put on coffee, let the Bug out back, and then went to the front porch for the paper. Simple stuff, but isn't that the substance of contentment? He sat at the breakfast table and his head became a thoroughfare for thoughts like, *Wash the car—nah. Go fishing—maybe.* But he just sat there in a pair of old shorts, reading the paper and sipping coffee: a good way to start the day.

Lethargic and thinking of things to do and then not doing them, he realized it was nice to be home. He had to laugh, thinking of Morey, though he knew Morey's would continue to have an adverse affect on his life for as long as they both worked in the same place.

But good things came from being home, even if it meant no pay. This week off could be a good opportunity to reconnect with who he thought he should be, or used to be, or could've been. He wanted to be someone with character and at least a modicum of virtuosity. He thought of his mother and his Catholic upbringing and her stories of saints and angels. Her characters displayed honesty, kindness and courage in the face of adversity. They inspired, but Jack had caved in to peer-pressure and the temptations of the flesh anyway. Drunkenness and lust had occupied him for many years, and now, despite being sober, he found that he couldn't live up to his own standards all the time. Most of the time? Any of the time?

Oh well, Jack thought. *Maybe I can look into going back to school or getting some kind of training that will get me away from Morey and the post office.*

The only person he would miss if he got out of there would be Julia.

She's beautiful, he told himself. *I wonder if she would consider going out with a gringo? Probably not, considering the bad hombre in the Camaro.*

He realized he was grinning: sitting at home and almost happy, just a little lonely.

Chapter 11

Before Jack had even gotten out of bed, in Fairfax, Sandi Andersen woke up for what seemed like the millionth time and felt as though she hadn't slept at all. She called United and told her supervisor that she had a family emergency and that she had been up all night.

"What seems to be the problem? Is there anything we can do?" her supervisor wanted to know.

"Well, no, there's nothing anyone can do right now; but thank you. I'll call back when I have more news."

"All right, but be sure to call this evening if you need off tomorrow. We'll need to schedule someone to cover for you."

The airline didn't tolerate absences well. Sandi didn't care. She didn't mind confrontation when she deemed it necessary. She held the lives of her co-workers in contempt, including her superiors.

She fixed tea and worried the whole time, but not about her job. She worried about Race, and even more she worried about herself.

What is he thinking? What's going on?

Part of her wanted to panic, but she persisted in anger mixed with her worry.

And where the hell is he? she wondered.

There had been no news at the hospitals. If Race were hurt—or worse—that would be terrible. If he weren't, that might not be so good either. She had secrets, and she knew from the beginning she and Race would not be together long. Last night probably meant the end.

She called Ellen.

Ellen picked up after one ring.

"Hello?" she said. Her voice sounded timid and tired.

"Hi, it's me. Any word from George?"

"No. I'm really getting frightened, Sandi. What should we do?" Ellen's emotions balanced on the threshold of an emotional black hole. If she crossed over there would be no return. Instinct or intuition told Sandi that Ellen shouldn't be alone.

I might be better off with other people around, too, she thought.

"Let me get dressed and I'll come over. Maybe we can get some help. At least we can keep each other company."

She hung up the phone, showered, and dressed. She fixed a piece of toast and drank some orange juice, then drove to George and Ellen's house. Or perhaps it was just Ellen's house, now. Sandi didn't know.

Ellen wore her grief like a like a spray of roses on a casket. It was the first time in 35 years that George hadn't come home or called.

"Let's call Eddie's wife, just to see if she's heard anything," Sandi said. "Do you know her number?"

"I have a phone number, but I don't know if it's any good," said Ellen. "Their number has changed a few times."

She sorted through a small, wooden box and pulled out an index card.

"I hope it's good," she said, and handed the phone number to Sandi.

She was clearly too upset and possibly too embarrassed to make the call herself.

"What's his wife's name?" Sandi asked, dialing and trying to keep her voice calm. "I don't think I've ever met her."

"It's Sharyl, spelled real funny."

The phone rang seven times and, as Sandi was about to hang up, an exasperated woman's voice said, "Hello?"

Then the receiver bounced on the floor or a table or something and a baby started crying. A blaring television battered the air with cartoons and grated with the sounds of cackling children.

After some fumbling, Sandi heard, "I'm sorry, hello? I dropped the phone."

"Um, this is Sandi Andersen. My Race rides to work with your Eddie and with George."

"I'm sorry Eddie didn't call, he's, uh..."

"But he's there?" Sandi's heart began a sprint that would surely end up outside her chest.

"Well, he's, uh, not here right now."

Sandi calmed a bit as she realized the woman's dilemma.

"Sharyl, I'm at George's house with Ellen. George and Race didn't come home last night either, and neither of them called. We called to see if you had seen or heard from Eddie since yesterday. We're worried sick. Can you help us?"

"Oh gosh, Sandi, I'm so sorry. Eddie didn't come home either, but I didn't think twice about it. Sometimes he stays, um, at, um, his mother's or somewhere."

"Could you try to locate him for us? And call back if you find him, okay? We'll do the same. Do you have George's phone number?"

"Um, I'm not sure. It must be here somewhere."

"Let me give it to you. Do you have something to write with?"

After a brief interlude Sharyl recorded the phone number. Sandi hung up and looked at Ellen. Ellen knew it wasn't good news.

"We've got to call the police," Sandi said.

She tried to insinuate sympathy, but her voice remained firm.

"I know," said Ellen, "but I hate to admit that it's come to this."

"Got a phone book?" Sandi asked. "I don't think we need 911."

Yet, she added to herself.

Race woke up in the motel. He felt stoned after the first sleep he had had since killing two people and finding his mother's corpse. He had slept surprisingly well, but he found himself dissatisfied. None of his problems had gone away. He still needed a lawyer; he still needed to avoid being recognized; and he still had a seething anger that had to be sated.

But first, he had to be vigilant and wary. The girl at the office had seen his ID, and she could describe him. If she was still there and still alone, he could fix that.

He showered quickly and got dressed. He tossed his belongings into his mother's car as he walked to the office. There he found the young woman, who was still at work and apparently still alone.

"Hey, uh, could you come look at something in the room? I don't want you to think I broke it, but somebody did," he said.

"Oh, hi, sure" she said, "I'll come look. I can't believe these people around here. We just had to paint in there and replace the mattress. What else did you find?"

They walked back to the room, her talking all the way, like she was on speed or drank too much coffee or both. Did she really think he gave a damn about her insipid life? Race was removing the gun from the small of his back as he allowed her to enter first.

"What is it you wanted to show me?" she asked, and turned to face him.

He threw her to the bed. She screamed and started to fight. She was afraid of being raped, but she needn't have been.

With strength fortified by adrenaline Race held her down, even as she kicked and clawed. He put a knee to her chest while he grabbed the pillow and pushed it into her face. Then he buried the gun in the pillow by her temple and squeezed the trigger.

There was noise, but not much. Her body went suddenly limp.

Race had another mess to clean up. This wasn't like the fights he had when he was younger. These people didn't limp or crawl away. They didn't leave at all. He would have to do something.

He rolled her up in the bedspread, pillow and all, and heaved her into the bathtub with its nicotine stains on the rim. He pulled the shower curtain closed, and then he headed back to the office.

Gotta be quick, he told himself.

He jumped the counter and opened the file box she had used the night before. He found the card with his name on it and stuffed it in his pocket. Then he took the paper money out of the register, $82. Another leap put him back over the counter and out the door.

It took all of his restraint to keep from sprinting. He didn't want to arouse the suspicion of anyone driving by. Even so, his brisk pace brought him to his mother's car in seconds. He fired the engine and shot out of the gravel lot. He sped down a hill and up another and checked his rear view mirror. A half-mile back an older Cadillac turned into the motel parking lot.

Surprise! Race thought, and then, *Got out of there just in time!*

He headed north on route 340. There wasn't anything on the news about bodies being found by the Beaver Dam Reservoir, so he should still be safe in Northern Virginia. He would call an attorney and get the clock ticking on the arrival of his fortune. Then he would find Sandi. He had to find Sandi.

Chapter 12

Sandi and Ellen tried to comfort each other, but mostly, Sandi comforted Ellen. George was a large portion of her life. He had been her husband for decades; he had fathered her children, shared her dreams, and shared her bed. Now, he was missing. She clung to hope, and she needed Sandi to help her deny her fears.

Race, on the other hand, had been part of Sandi's life for two years. They shared a house, a bed and the enhanced lifestyle of two incomes. Sandi was worried all right, but her uneasiness paled in comparison to the devastation that tormented Ellen. Sandi could go on. Ellen could not. She might continue to breathe, but she could not go on.

"Let me fix you some more tea," Sandi said.

"No, Sandi, thank you," Ellen replied. "I just wish the police could do something other than file a report. Why aren't they looking for them?"

"I suppose they know what they're doing," Sandi said. Then, because she couldn't stand just waiting anymore, she said "Why don't we see if we can find out anything from the foreman out in Aldie? Do you know where the houses are that they were working on?"

"Not really," Ellen said. "Is there someone we could call?"

"I don't know," Sandi said, "but we can probably find the work site. How much new construction can there be in Aldie?" She hoped that getting Ellen out would help. It could be good for both of them. And maybe in the meantime the guys would show up.

Race drove back to Front Royal and then eastbound on I-66. From there it took about forty-five minutes to drive to Centreville. From Centreville he could call an attorney, but whom? Not a firm, or at least not a large one. He still craved anonymity. Some small part of him, buried in his tortured psyche, was ashamed of what he had done, but he felt more fear than shame: fear of being caught.

He got off the interstate at exit 52, the first Centreville exit, and onto Route 29. He took an immediate right and another right and pulled into the parking lot in front of the Centreville branch of the Fairfax County Public Library. A pay phone stood by the sidewalk near the entrance, exposed, but only to a few library users. The rest of the parking lot was shielded by a solid row of conifers reaching raggedly toward the sky.

He parked in the midst of a bunch of cars and walked to the phone. Two phone books were still attached, somewhat of a miracle considering the widespread vandalism in rapidly growing Northern Virginia. He opened the yellow book to 'attorneys' and began scanning. Many firms were listed. He skipped over them, looking for a single-attorney private practice. There were a few, but most had addresses he recognized from the business part of Fairfax, near the courthouse. He didn't particularly want to go there—only if he had to.

There! William Echols!

Echols was listed in a residential neighborhood, not too far from town, but far enough.

Race dropped two quarters into the slot and dialed.

The phone rang five times before a man answered, "Echols law."

"William Echols, please," Race replied. It felt funny to speak. It was the first time he had spoken to a person since the girl at the motel this morning.

"This is William Echols, what can I do for you?" came the reply.

"I need someone to handle a legal matter for me, and I want to remain anonymous. Can you do that?" Race asked.

"I can within the confines of the law," said Echols. "What's the situation you want handled anonymously?"

"Its legal, I just don't want anyone to know. Not anyone, understand?" It was more a threat than a question.

William Echols, PC, would not be cowed over the phone. "And your name, sir, which will remain anonymous?"

"I have a lottery ticket worth eleven-million dollars. I want the money, and I don't want anyone to know I have it. Can we do that?"

Echols knew about the unclaimed Virginia Lottery money. He had heard about it on the radio that very morning. Visions of 35% of a settlement in a law suit leapt into Echols head, but this wasn't a settlement. That notwithstanding, how smart was this guy on the phone?

"Yeah, we can do that," said Echols. "Do you want to pay attorney's fees up front, or shall I just count on a portion of the winnings?"

"I'll give you $500 up front. Will it cost any more than that?" Race asked.

Damn! Echols thought, but he said, "It depends on how much time I need to spend getting the proceeds."

Something is better than nothing, he thought.

"If it comes to more, I can wait until you have the money. With eleven-million, I know you'll be good for it."

"How much more could it cost?" Race asked. He was getting angry; someone was trying to take what was his. The ire in his voice gave rise to a pause in William Echols thinking.

"I charge $300 an hour. I don't think I will need to spend more than five or six hours getting your money."

"Five or six!"

Anger welled up in Race. The chemistry and emotion of the previous day and the following morning reasserted themselves.

"Well, we need a contract, and, of course, I will have to actually go get the money. We can't do this through the mail you know. The officials will want to examine the ticket, and I'm sure you won't want me to let it out of my sight. I'll have to wait until they are satisfied to get the winnings. Then, of course, we need to get together, or I can deposit the money in a bank of your choice."

"How do we get this started?" Race asked. Resignation had replaced his rage.

"I'll need the ticket," said Echols. "We can draw up a codicil stating that the ticket and the proceeds belong to you and that I am simply acting in your behalf."

"How do I know you won't take the money?"

"You will have a copy of the ticket and a copy of our agreement. Just sue me if I take the money. But I won't, sir. I have a good practice, a good income, and I don't want to leave the country," he said, but he thought, *These yokels can be real morons.*

"How long is this going to take?" Race was in a hurry.

"I can see you tomorrow at two," Echols said. *That should give me time for lunch with Deborah after court,* he thought.

"What's wrong with now?" Race demanded.

"Sir, I have to be in court in 30 minutes. Besides, we need a contract. I'll have my secretary type it today, and we'll have it tomorrow."

"What's wrong with this afternoon?"

"Sir, I have other clients," Echols said. *And you're only paying me $1800 out of $11 million, you cheapskate.*

"I'll pay," said Race.

"So will my other clients," said Echols.

"So I'll pay double," Race replied. He needed this done.

Now you're talkin'! thought Echols, whose only appointment that afternoon was with a barstool at TT Reynolds.

"I'll see what I can do," said Echols. "Can you call me back at, say, one o'clock?"

"No," said Race. "I'll be at your office. You're on University Drive, right?"

"Yeah, yeah, University Drive. What's your name?"

"Why?" asked Race.

"The contract," replied Echols. "I need to have it on the contract."

There was a pause, and finally, "John Racine Hardin. Yeah, like in Wisconsin. No, no 'g.' Just H-A-R-D-I-N, Hardin." Race returned the phone to its hook.

Chapter 13

The phone startled Jack, erupting as it did in the silence, snatching his attention and yanking him back to reality. He had just walked in from washing his car, and he grabbed a Diet Coke from the fridge. It wouldn't do much to hydrate him, but it felt good going down, and it tasted good.

"Oh, what the hell," he said aloud, "I'll answer it," and grabbed the receiver. It was only a few feet away, hanging on the kitchen wall.

"Hello," Jack said.

"I need some answers," said Morey.

"Why don't you just make some up," Jack replied. "Isn't that what you usually do?"

"You're in more trouble than you bargained for, wise guy. Somebody from Social Security phoned, and he wants answers. I told him I'd have you on the carpet today at 1 o'clock. Be on time, for a change!"

"I don't know if that fits my schedule, Morey. The newspaper is really thick today. Why don't we just do this next week when you're paying me?"

"You're going to find yourself in jail if you don't watch it," Morey threatened. "These people aren't fooling around."

"They are if they're talking to you, Morey," Jack said. "What's this all about anyway?"

"Just be here," Morey ordered. "The postmaster says you'll get paid for coming in."

Then Jack heard a 'click' and a dial tone.

Paid for it? I guess I'll be there.

"They didn't show yesterday or today," the foreman said. "Kind of unusual for them. Any other contractor, it wouldn't surprise me."

He looked at the two women and asked, "Any trouble? Somethin' I could help you with?"

Normally he wouldn't bother with someone else's problems, but these two, the older woman especially, looked worried and lost. He had to offer. It was the least he could do. Besides, the younger one was kind of attractive.

"No, unless you happen to see them, you know, if they show up," Sandi said. "We need to locate them. Can I give you my cell phone number?"

"Sure," he said, trying not to sound eager.

She didn't want to tell him that George, Race and Eddie hadn't been home. It felt too private, a dark, little secret.

After leaving their contact information with the job foreman, and an affirmation of the importance of locating the men, Sandi and Ellen started back to Fairfax.

"They missed work both days," Ellen said. "George wouldn't do that."

"We'll find out what happened," said Sandi, and she knew they would, but she didn't know if Ellen would like it.

Race parked his mother's car at Dulles in the long-term parking and took the shuttle to the terminal. He began his search for Sandi at the United Airlines check-in counters. She wasn't there but he waited for several minutes to see if she would show up, maybe to relieve someone or to open another check-in station. He didn't want to talk to anyone unless he had to.

After what seemed a long time, he left and went down to the baggage carousels. The place was dead. A uniformed employee of United was near the information booth looking at tags on unclaimed luggage, but it wasn't Sandi. It was a man. His nametag read A. Gardner. He was about ten years older than Race.

Race didn't want to look any further. He would have to ask this guy where Sandi was working. He walked over to the booth and stood. Al Gardner noticed him almost immediately.

"Hi, can I help you?"

"I'm looking for Sandi Andersen," Race replied. "I'm supposed to meet her here somewhere, but I'm not sure where."

The man's look gave away his thoughts: *Should I give this guy any information about her? Is it any of his business?*

After hesitating he said, "She took today off. You sure you were supposed to meet here?" He looked hard at Race.

"I must've got my signals crossed," Race said, then hung his head and walked away, not an easy thing for him to do.

I should have known, he told himself, and continued walking.

He turned right and walked down to an exit. He came out where the shuttles picked up passengers to go back to the satellite parking areas and other places. He caught one going to the car rental agencies.

Sandi and Ellen returned to Ellen's kitchen where Sandi fixed sandwiches, even though Ellen claimed she was not hungry.

"It'll be good for you," Sandi said. "You've got to eat."

A little burgundy Toyota Corolla zipped into the last parking place just as Jack pulled into the employee's parking lot at the Fairfax Post Office.

This place is cursed! Jack thought. Then he noticed whose car had beaten him to the last space. *Maybe not.* A smile played on his lips.

Julia got out of her car and was about to hurry back into the post office when she noticed Jack, sitting in his idling Chevy, smiling as big as the windshield. She smiled, looked at her car, and then back at Jack.

"Sorry," she yelled, but a telling grin and a one shoulder shrug belied her veracity.

"Doesn't seniority count for anything anymore?" Jack yelled back through his open window.

"No," Julia replied, "You're on vacation, remember?"

"Yeah, right. Hold on a second I'll walk in with you."

"I'm late Jack. I had to pick up my car for lunch, and it took too long."

"Whose car is that next to yours? Larry's right? He won't get off until four or later," Jack said and parked broadside behind Julia and the other car. "There, that didn't take long did it?"

Julia looked like she was being tickled and trying not to laugh.

"You are crazy, you know that?" she said. "Loco."

"Or stupid," Jack replied, "but this is the post office. Being stupid shouldn't be a problem. I might even get promoted."

They walked side by side toward the back door of the building.

"What are you doing here?" Julia asked.

"I wanted to see if you were still riding to work with that tough hombre in the Camaro," Jack said.

"El hombrote just took me to pick up my car," Julia responded in a mocking tone of voice.

"Oh, so he's your go to guy, huh? What's the matter? My car not good enough for you?" Julia gave him a quizzical look. Then a little light came on.

"He's my brother, and you were jealous, Jack! You were jealous!"

She laughed and bumped him playfully with her hip. Jack's embarassment flooded his face.

"Of course, I was jealous. You're the most beautiful woman in the world and you were with some other guy," Jack said.

"Oh, yeah, right!" She replied. "And don't you love my outfit today? Slightly dirty jeans and a T-shirt? Quite a fashion statement, wouldn't you say?"

"It's beautiful," Jack said, in a perfect imitation of sincerity.

Then they were inside.

"I gotta go, Jack. Come tell me before you leave, why you are here, okay?"

"Yeah, I will," he said and began missing her immediately.

The thirty-second love affair, Jack thought, *my specialty. And brother or not, he didn't look particularly happy about seeing Julia with me.*

Jack forced thoughts of Julia out of his head as he walked toward the front office. He could see the postmaster talking to a man in a gray, three-piece suit and Morey standing beside them trying to look like he was part of the discussion. He wasn't.

Jack knocked on the open door and walked in. All eyes turned toward him and he wished he had dressed a little better.

Maybe I should have worn something other than jeans, he thought, but he said, "You needed to see me?"

He addressed the postmaster and, for the time being, ignored the other two men in the room.

The postmaster responded coolly. He and Jack had never had a problem firsthand, but Morey's harassment and accompanying paperwork overflowed onto the postmaster's desk, and Jack's name came up too often in a negative way.

"Jack, this is Mr. Einstein from the Social Security Administration. He has a few questions he would like to ask, if you don't mind."

"No, I don't mind," Jack said, and he looked at Einstein.

"Alright then, we'll leave you two alone," the postmaster said, and he turned to leave.

Morey had no choice but to follow his boss, like a gross mathematical error following a perfect equation. The door closed behind Jack.

"Those two seem to think you're in trouble," said Einstein. "Is that normal around here?"

Jack laughed. "Pretty much."

"I just need a little help," Einstein said. "I'd like to know if you have been delivering a Social Security check to a certain address, and if so, I'd like to know the names of all the individuals receiving mail there. The address is 319 Maple Street."

Jack ran the houses on Maple through his memory and then the checks he had been delivering on the 3rd of every month for years.

"Yeah, I get a check every month for Thelma Hardin. That's the only piece of mail she ever gets there. There's some guy there named John Hardin and a woman named Sandra Andersen. I just figured John was the son and Thelma was in a nursing home or something."

Einstein wrote as he spoke. "And you delivered a check this month? Yesterday, specifically?" Einstein asked.

"Sure did. Late in the day, as I recall," Jack said, as if he might have forgotten. We had a postal screw up with a tray of mail, and some of your guys' checks didn't get here until yesterday afternoon. I wasn't supposed to hold on to that, was I?" Jack wondered if maybe Morey had set him up.

"No, no. You did the right thing. As a matter of fact, thanks for the extra effort. Your supervisor said you made a second trip. For some reason, he sounded like that was a bad thing, you know, your fault."

One side of Einstein's lip went up, and a question sparkled in his eyes.

Jack laughed again and said, "If it involves me, Morey pretty much thinks it's a bad thing and it's my fault."

Einstein smiled. "Thanks for your help, Jack," he said, and offered his hand.

Chapter 14

Race parked his rental on University Drive in Fairfax and walked to Echols' door.

"Come in." He heard, some voice bellowing out of the split-level before him, "Down the stairs and to your right."

Race opened the door and walked in.

"I saw you pull up," the voice said from a room half a flight down. "You must be Mr. Harding."

"Hardin," Race said.

He walked down the stairs and peered into a disheveled office occupied by a disheveled man.

"Sit down, Mr. Hardin. I'm Bill Echols."

The man half rose and offered his hand.

Race reached over to shake Bill Echols' hand and sat in the chair in front of the desk. The two men went over a contract that Echols' had typed, and Race checked the spelling of his name. It was correct.

"Why does it take so many words," he wanted to know. "This is a simple agreement."

"The law is like that," Echols assured him. "That's just the way it has to be. If I were going to cash your paycheck for you we would have the same arrangement. It would be your money, and I'd be acting on your behalf."

Race thought of his mother's Social Security check. He thought of how many times he had signed that check, acting with power of attorney, and handed it to Sandi. Race signed the agreement with Echols, but not without some hesitation.

"Now," said Echols, "let's get the ball rolling. I'm sure you want your money. This shouldn't take long. I need the ticket, Mr. Harding."

"It's Hardin," Race said, and gave Echols a hard look, a look like the ticket would remain in his pocket.

"I'm going to have to have it, Mr. Hardin. There's no other way to get this done."

"I've got the ticket," Race said, "right here."

He reached in his back pocket and pulled out his wallet. He removed the ticket and held it out but didn't let go when Echols grasped the end.

"I want you to make a copy. I'll go with you when you are ready to get the money."

Race looked squarely into the attorney's eyes.

"I'm not going to jerk you around, Mr. Hardin, I assure you."

Bill Echols took the ticket and checked the number against the winning number he had retrieved from the newspaper.

"We have a winner," he said, imitating a bingo caller and falling short of being amusing.

But he held a ticket worth $11 million, and for a second he wanted to bolt and never return. Greed had a way of gripping a person and wresting away every vestige of integrity they ever possessed. Compulsive greed actually made Echols' hands shake. But running and not returning unnerved him, especially with Race Hardin leveling an intimidating glare at him. He couldn't act spontaneously; he needed a plan, and he didn't have one. The moment passed. He made a copy of the ticket.

"Let's give the lottery commission a call, let 'em know there's a winner," Echols said. "An anonymous winner."

Hammond and Riley had the name of the woman whose death they were investigating, the old woman in the rocker, but, before the investigation went any further, someone discovered another body. This time a young woman had been killed in a motel on Route 340 near Front Royal.

"I guess there'll be another soon," said Riley. "Don't these come in three's?"

John Hammond just looked at him, that look he had that disquieted so many, but it didn't faze Riley. The two had been partners for a long time.

"The old woman can wait," Riley continued. "She's waited this long. Let's go get whoever did the motel job. The first on the scene are calling it robbery."

Hammond kept staring; Riley simply looked back. He knew that behind the eyes turned the wheels of science and detection.

Finally, Hammond said, "Murder. Kind of extreme for not much money; there couldn't have been much in that little cracker box of a motel. Doesn't seem right. Let's get out there."

They drove to the motel and found Hammond's intuition correct. Something wasn't right. People don't usually kill during a simple robbery. And why was the body in room two, not room one or any of the other rooms? Why not in the office? While the techs lifted prints and collected evidence, Hammond and Riley went through the files in the office.

"No record of anyone spending the night, but someone killed her in room two. Was it rape? Someone she knew? Lovers? No sign of a struggle getting to the room. Why room two?" Riley exploded with questions. In his chosen profession, that was a good thing.

"Let's look at room two again," Hammond said. "I think someone slept there. Somebody could have spent the night there, whether there's a record or not. The towels were used."

By the time Hammond and Riley got back to their barracks, they had evidence: hair, several sets of fingerprints, and a plaster mold of a tire track from the parking lot outside the office. They also had a message from Thelma Hardin's phone, a new message. One of the techs had gone back in the morning to pick up some items he had left and heard the call. It was from the Social Security Administration, someone named Einstein. He wanted a call back.

"Einstein," said Riley. "I wonder if Sherlock Holmes is going to get in on the act, too."

"Just call him," Hammond replied. He had that look on his face again, the thinking, often mistaken for threatening, look.

Within minutes, Einstein and Riley knew they were involved in a Social Security scam. Thelma Hardin had been dead for months, but her check still arrived at the address on Maple Street in Fairfax uninterrupted.

"And you haven't been able to contact anyone at that address?" Riley spoke into the phone. Then, after a pause, "Yeah, we'll be all over it. I'll let you know what we come up with."

He hung up and turned to Hammond and said, "We gotta find out who lives at this address on Maple Street in Fairfax. And who is this George Reiss guy, and what's his truck doing at Thelma's?"

"And find Thelma's car and talk to everyone who knows the woman at the motel," Hammond added. "Do you suppose Thelma's doer came back for the car, or maybe someone stumbled onto the situation and took the only thing there of any value?"

"I think someone could have bought a car with Thelma's check," Riley said. "And if the doer was George Reiss, why did he leave a perfectly good pick-up and take an old car?"

"Let's call him and ask," said Hammond.

They spoke to Ellen, who had hoped they had information for her. Instead she gave information to them.

"We'll contact Fairfax County, then, ma'am," Riley said.

He hung up the phone and looked at Hammond.

"The guy's missing, and his wife didn't like where we found his truck. She said she can't imagine what it was doing there."

It was Hammond's turn. He picked up the phone and called the Fairfax County Police.

"You have a missing person, George Reiss…" he said, and they exchanged information.

Hammond hung up the phone and said, "Now, let's see who lives on Maple Street."

Both men headed for the door.

Ellen called her children. Her son was coming in the morning if George hadn't shown up by then. Eddie's wife, Sharyl, called. She said she couldn't come over because of the children. She conceded that even Eddie would have called by now. Sandi's nerves began to fray. She wanted to get away from the emotionally charged atmosphere surrounding Ellen and Sharyl. She needed time to take an objective look at the situation. It could change her life. Where was Race? What was he thinking? She should have heard from him by now, unless...she left the thought unfinished.

♠

Jack found Julia in the lobby replacing locks on boxes no longer in use, waiting to be rented again.

"So, why are you here?" she asked. "I thought you were on 'vacation' because Morey likes you so much."

"Talking to some guy looking for some guy," Jack replied. "I could have done this over the phone, but I guess they wanted to see me. Maybe they thought I did something wrong, I don't know."

They talked, just to be talking and time flew. Finally, they heard someone yelling from outside:

"Who the hell parked behind my car?"

"Uh oh," Julia said and smiled.

"Oops," said Jack.

"You better go move your car. I have to punch out," Julia said.

They separated slowly, reluctance pulling at them like gravity, as if they each embodied more mass than the planet.

Outside, Jack apologized: "Sorry, Larry. Lost track of time."

"Time, hell, Jack. This is my time. What makes you so special, anyway."

"Calm down, Larry. The 7-11 will still have a six-pack when you get there." Jack glanced back as he got in the Chevy and noticed another Chevrolet cruising into the lot, a Camaro. He fired the engine, but the other car pulled up behind him.

"What the F—!" Larry muttered, but he didn't confront the man in the Camaro.

Jack leaned out his window, arm hanging out the door and turned as far as he could to look at the other driver. It was the 'tough hombre' and he was head, arm and shoulder out of his hot rod.

"You know Julia, right? I saw you with her yesterday."

Jack projected calmness, but his 'fight or flight' instinct stirred. *I don't think it's going to be flight,* he thought. *I'm blocked in.*

"Yeah, I know her," he said.

"Can you guys discuss this some other time," Larry offered and both of the other men looked at him.

Looking back at Jack, Angel said, "She inside? She's late. I wanna be sure she's okay. How come you're parked behind her car?"

Julia walked out of the building toward them.

"Geez!" Larry said to no one in particular.

"What's going on?" Julia asked as she approached the three men.

Angel rattled off a paragraph in Spanish, and Julia returned one.

"Alright, I'll see you tonight," Angel said and looked right at Jack.

The Camaro's tires chirped as it started to back out of the parking lot, but they screeched to a halt as the unmarked sedan of Riley and Hammond pulled in.

"Give me a break!" Larry continued his muttering.

Angel honked his horn. "Hey!"

Riley was about to pop the cruiser in reverse when he hesitated. "I know you, don't I?"

Angel recognized the detectives. He got out of the Camaro and walked back to where they sat.

"I hope your friend isn't in trouble," Jack said to Julia.

"I'm sure he can take care of himself," she answered.

A smirk played across her face.

Angel looked up from leaning on the door of the State-owned car and hollered, "Hey, Julia. Who lives at 319 Maple Street?"

Julia used to sort mail to the carriers before she became the box-section clerk. After only a moment's thought, she realized Jack carried the mail on Maple Street. She looked at Jack with raised eyebrows. Jack looked at her and then back toward the men in the car.

"Who wants to know?" he asked, opening the door of his car and starting back toward the cruiser.

"Who are you?" Riley asked, and flashed his badge.

Jack sauntered to the vehicle and stood beside Angel. A palpable sizing up of each other ensued as Jack spoke:

"Jack Casey. I deliver mail on Maple Street."

"You got a funny uniform. I thought Maple Street was in the City of Fairfax," Riley replied. "Don't you guys have to wear uniforms?"

"I'm off today," Jack explained. "I had to come in to talk to someone about a delivery." Then he thought, *Cops always put you on the defensive. How do they do that?*

"We need all the information you can give us about the person or persons at the address on Maple."

"You just missed some guy from the Social Security Admin looking for the same info," Jack said.

"Yeah, I spoke to him an hour or so ago," Riley's voice inflected familiarity. "Is there somewhere we can talk?"

After some vehicular juggling, the cruiser got parked, Larry finally got out and Jack pulled into the now empty spot by Julia's car.

Angel looked at Julia before backing out. "You okay?" he asked.

"Yes, I'm okay," she said.

She looked a little embarrassed. "I gotta go," she said to Jack. Her eyes darted to his and back to the pavement. She moved to the driver's side of her car and got in.

Jack looked away from Julia and over at Angel. Angel was looking back at him.

Chapter 15

Race walked out the front door of Echols' split-foyer and hopped into the rental car. He drove to a shopping center near the historic district of Fairfax and used a pay phone to call Sandi's bungalow. He listened to the phone ring until the answering machine started its message. He hung up.

Sandi left Ellen with promises to call and headed home. She needed time to think. An onslaught of questions tortured her. Where was Race? Why did he and George and Eddie disappear? It must have something to do with the three of them, but what? Were they alive? Were they still together? She couldn't help but think that Race had done something, and not that something had been done to him. She needed to know. But first she needed to be safe. Instead of driving back to her house, Sandi headed to the Seven-Eleven near it.

Hammond and Riley took what little information Jack could give them and headed for 319 Maple Street. They pulled up in front of the bungalow, swung open the doors of the cruiser and started across the yard. The house looked empty and felt empty. They noticed a small, red car driving by with no passengers, just a man driving. Neither one of them thought twice about it.

Cops, Race thought, as they watched him pass. *Wasting everybody's time, as usual, knocking on doors at empty houses.*

His small rental had to be red. The only damned cheap car left on the lot. He had hoped for something more forgettable.

There's no going back to that place now. But where's Sandi? She's not at work or at home. Is she looking for me, or running?

He wheeled the little red rental out of his old neighborhood. He would call Echols later and see how much longer it would take to get his eleven million dollars. Meanwhile, he would hunt for Sandi. He needed to find her. He needed to find her soon.

After concluding the interview with Hammond and Riley, Jack headed home.

Julia, Julia, Jack thought. *We could be just right for each other. Or do you think I'm too white? Ah, well, some things just aren't meant to be. But, maybe...*

His thoughts went on; his mood rose and fell as he thought about what could have been or ought to be. Or maybe still could be. He pulled into a Seven-Eleven for a diet Coke, not that he was on a diet; he had simply become addicted to the taste back when he quit drinking and started eating again. His waist had started to grow so he began drinking diet Coke. He had his waist under control now, but not the diet Coke.

He parked beside a Porsche and walked into the store. A familiar looking blonde passed him in the aisle on his way to the cooler in the back.

"Excuse me," she said in a not unfriendly manner as she tried to get around him in the narrow aisle.

"No problem," Jack replied and stepped to the side.

I know her, he thought.

Jack saw so many people in a day, sometimes he didn't recognize the people who lived on his route unless he saw them in context. He knew that he knew them; he just couldn't remember who they were. Sometimes an entire day would pass before he figured out who they were.

She must live on my route. I wouldn't forget meeting her somewhere else.

He grabbed a 20-ounce bottle of diet Coke and made his way up to the front. A man at the counter wanted lots of lottery tickets, and he wanted specific numbers. The blonde stood behind the man, waiting, holding a bottle of some kind of spring water and some travel-sized toiletries. Jack fell in line behind her.

"Time consuming isn't it?" he said.

The woman half turned and smiled.

"I'm sorry," Jack said, "I don't mean to be forward, but don't I know you from somewhere? I deliver mail in Fairfax and you look so familiar I thought maybe I'd seen you before."

The guy buying lottery tickets was still rattling off numbers. The woman turned all the way around.

"Maybe," she said. "I live in Fairfax, but I work out at Dulles, so I'm usually not home during the day. Where do you deliver mail?"

Jack named some neighborhoods, and she confided that she did live in one of them.

"Sandi," she said. "Sandi Anderson, and she held out her hand.

"Oh yeah," Jack said, and *Oh crap!* he thought, remembering Einstein, Hammond and Reilly. And then he said, "Jack Casey. I deliver your mail."

They shook hands and, despite himself, Jack liked the softness and warmth. He had a hard time believing state and federal officials wanted information about her, presumably in connection with shady dealings.

"You don't really remember where I live, do you?" she said coyly.

Jack laughed. "I do," he said. "How could I forget where someone like you lives?"

"A minute ago you didn't even know where you knew me from," she accused.

She's cute, Jack thought and smiled. *Maybe she's not a felon!* As if looks would make a difference.

"I don't suppose you've seen my roommate around," Sandi said.

"No, not lately. Besides, him I could forget."

"Me, too," she replied, rolling her eyes, "but I think I have to deal with him at least one more time."

"I'm sorry," Jack said. "Anything I can do to help?" It was a rhetorical question, but, within reason, he would help someone if he could.

"Next," the cashier interrupted.

"Oops! Sandi spun and dropped a tiny tube of toothpaste and a hairbrush on the floor.

"I'll get it," Jack said as he lowered himself toward the floor. Sandi had crouched as well, and their hands touched again.

"Thanks," she said, her hand remaining on Jack's.

"No problem," Jack muttered, staring at the floor.

Sandi stood up and paid and, as she left, she said, "Bye, Jack. See you later."

Jack said, "Okay, Sandi," and she was out the door before he paid the cashier.

Very attractive, he thought, *and somehow very scary.*

He walked out to his car and saw Sandi standing by the Porsche.

"Actually, Jack, maybe you could help me. Do you have a few minutes?"

"Yeah, sure, Sandi," Jack said. *Scary,* he thought. *Really scary.*

"That guy I *used* to live with," she found it easy to say, "he kinda scares me. Could you drive by my house with me?"

"Sure," Jack said, *And why not?* he thought. *Julia's brother looks like he wants to kill me. What's one more?*

"Can we take your car?" Sandi asked. "He'd recognize mine."

"I bet he would," Jack said, admiring the Porsche. "It's a hard one not to recognize."

Julia and Angel sat on the balcony of their apartment at Shenandoah Crossings. The city had come to the suburbs, and they overlooked a four-lane highway, an office building and a high-end strip mall. Angel had a beer. It was his day off, and a hot one. He had run errands most of the day, and then he had checked on Julia to be sure she had gotten her car. That had been when he saw her with Jack for the second time.

"You embarrass me sometimes," Julia was saying. "Jack is a good guy."

"I just want to be sure," Angel replied. "I need to know you are safe. There are too many bad people around."

"I know," Julia said and rose. "I want some iced tea," she said. "May I get you another beer?"

"No. Well, yes. It's my day off, right?"

"Yes my brother, it is," Julia said with a mock sense of exasperation.

She put her hands on the either side of his head, tilted it back and kissed his forehead. She slid the screen door open and went in, returning momentarily with their drinks.

"You like this guy, Jack?" Angel asked.

"Why do you say that?" Julia's smile betrayed her feelings.

"I've seen you with him twice, and I can read body language, you know. I can read facial expressions, too," Angel teased, but part of him evinced concern.

"Is this my overprotective, state trooper bodyguard speaking?" she teased him right back.

"Oh no," he said. "It's far worse than that. This es tu Latino hermano speaking. We are family."

Julia laughed and said, "Jack is okay. He's my friend."

"And you like him, cierto o falso?"

"No."

"Yes."

They both laughed.

Chapter 16

No one answered their knock, so Hammond and Riley turned to leave the house on Maple Street. As they turned, Jack and Sandi approached in Jack's car.

"Who are they?" Sandi asked Jack, "Police?"

"I recognize them," Jack said. "They questioned me at the post office."

"About the guys being missing?" Sandi asked.

"No, something else," Jack said, and kept looking at the two men on the porch as he pulled into Sandi's driveway. They looked back.

"Isn't that our mailman?" Riley asked his partner.

They stood on the old concrete porch and Riley looked at Hammond. Hammond stared at the old Chevrolet. Jack and Sandi got out and approached the porch.

Riley looked at Sandi while he fumbled for his shield.

"Virginia State Police," he said. "And you are...?"

She stood with one hand on the hot, iron handrail and one foot on the first step. Looking up at the men, she felt servile even though she stood in front of her own house. Her pitch rose and her speech accelerated.

"Sandi, Sandi Anderson," she replied. "I live here. Are you here about Race? I don't have any idea where he is, or George or Eddie."

"And 'Race' is...?" Riley let the question hang in the air.

"We reported it, me and Ellen. Isn't that why you're here?"

"Could we come in and talk?" Hammond offered. "We need your help, and maybe we can help you," he said, and he and Riley exchanged glances.

Sandi walked up the steps between the two detectives. Jack waited at the bottom of the steps. The porch looked a little crowded. Sandi unlocked the door and showed the men into her living room. Hammond and Riley allowed Jack to walk between them and enter first, an act more subjugating than polite. They sat down in the dark, musty room, Jack on the couch, and Hammond and Riley in the overstuffed chair and the recliner. Neither one of them leaned back.

"Can I offer you something to drink? I can fix coffee, or something cooler," Sandi said.

The three men declined.

After twenty minutes and about the same number of questions, Riley and Hammond had gotten the gist of what was happening. Sandi, Ellen and Sharyl had reported that the three men in their lives had not been seen for over 24 hours, and the police now considered them officially missing.

"And none of them showed up at work yesterday or today," Hammond concluded.

He and Riley looked at each other and then at Jack.

"And, Mr. Casey, you didn't mention that you and Ms. Anderson knew each other."

They watched Jack squirm. Their looks were non-committal, but an accusation infused the statement.

"We just met," Jack replied. His attempt at nonchalance suffered with insincerity. "I stopped at a 7-11 and we ended up waiting in line together. I recognized Sandi and struck up a conversation," Jack said. And then he thought, *Damn! I'm on the defensive again! How do these guys do that?*

"And you gave her a ride home?" Riley asked.

"I was afraid," Sandi blurted out.

"Afraid of what?" Hammond asked immediately.

"You don't know Race," Sandi said, now on the verge of nervous tears.

"Why would he want to hurt you?" Riley asked with a hint of compassion.

"I don't know! I don't know!" Sandi sobbed. "I don't know where he is or why he disappeared."

She leaned into Jack, tears dampening his shirt. He reluctantly removed his arm from between them and put it around her.

"Do you know John Hardin's mother, Thelma Hardin?" Hammond broached the subject.

"No!" Sandi answered, and then added, "I know she lives out in the country. Race gets her...he takes care of her. She's old."

Jack sheepishly removed his arm from around Sandi's shoulders.

Hammond and Riley looked at each other.

"Okay. We'll be in touch," Riley said. "Call if anything new develops."

Standing, he handed Sandi his card. Then the two detectives walked out.

Back in the oven-like car, Riley turned the key and blasted the air conditioner with the windows down to blow the stifling air out.

Then he turned to Hammond and asked, "Where to, big guy?"

Hammond looked at Sandi's living room window as he replied, "Office. I want to see what we got on this guy, John Racine Hardin, and on Sandi Anderson and Jack Casey. Something isn't right here. She was way too nervous. And she was afraid of Hardin. What makes her think he's alive? She should be worried about what happened to him, not what he might do if he didn't get himself killed." He took a breath. "Then we can contact Ellen Reiss and Sharyl what's her name."

"Office it is," Riley said and put the car in gear.

Jack and Sandi sat together on the couch. She needed comfort, but Jack didn't like being so close to her right now. Was she grieving or just scared? Besides, they had just met. And what about Julia? Not that he owed Julia any allegiance, much less an explanation. Still, he felt like a trust had been broken, though none had been established.

It's nothing, Julia, he thought as an attractive, petite woman leaned into him seeking protection and warmth.

What the hell is wrong with me? Jack asked himself.

"Jack," Sandi said, taking his hand, "I'm afraid to stay here. Will you wait while I pack some clothes?"

"Do you really think that guy, your boyfriend, will hurt you? You don't even know what's happened yet."

"I know, I know," she said, "but I just don't feel comfortable. Race is...I just don't feel comfortable. Sometimes he just isn't right."

"Maybe you should've told the detectives that," Jack said.

"I can't," Sandi answered. "Maybe he's hurt or...well, maybe something happened. I don't want them thinking anything bad...but I'm still afraid."

Hammond and Riley never made it back to the office.

"...see the fisherman by the Beaver Dam Reservoir," the radio squawked.

"Two more bodies," Riley said. "Do you believe this? They're dropping like flies."

Chapter 17

After Sandi had packed enough clothes to last a couple of nights, she and Jack put her suitcase in the back of his car and headed back to the 7-11 to get the Porsche. Jack's mind stayed in high gear wondering where *Sandi* would be sleeping.

Does she want to stay with me? Should I ask? Is she going to ask? Am I supposed to help her? Do I want to help her? Mom? No answer.

When he and Sandi arrived at the 7-11 Jack asked, "Do you have somewhere to go, a friend's house or something?"

Sandi turned toward him. She put her hand on his arm.

"I don't know, Jack. I was thinking of a motel. No one would know where I was."

"Oh, yeah, of course."

Jack looked at her. He truly felt sorry for her, but he didn't know what to do with her.

Should I just let her go to a motel, or offer to help, or what? C'mon, Mom. What do I do?

"But, it is a lot of money, staying in a motel." Her hand still rested on his arm. "Do you have a place? Could I stay on your couch or something? I wouldn't want to be in the way, but…" she burst into tears.

She clutched Jack's arm with both hands now and leaned into his shirt, sobbing.

"It's okay, Sandi. I have a house. I mean, it's just a little one, but big enough for two. My wife and I…ex-wife, my ex-wife. I mean, no one else is there. It'd just be the two of us. I mean, there's plenty of room."

Jack's thoughts vacillated between, *What have I gotten myself into?* and, *Are there any clean sheets in the house?*

Sandi snuffled and stopped crying. She even laughed a little as Jack left shoeprints all over his tongue trying to get his foot out of his mouth. Her laugh relieved some of Jack's tension, at least for the moment.

He might be just what I need, Sandi thought, *at least for a little while.*
She slid her left hand down Jack's arm and held his hand.
"I won't be any trouble," she said, and she smiled.
"Just follow me," Jack said, and he leaned over her to open her door.
Sandi gently turned his face toward her and kissed him.
"Thank you, Jack."

Race had driven out toward Dulles and back looking for Sandi. The amount of traffic made it difficult to look for one individual, even one in a Porsche. He headed back to Fairfax and was about to turn into the subdivision where Sandi lived, when he saw a Porsche pull out of the 7-11.

Not many of those around, he thought. *This should be her.*
Race scrutinized the car and, as it turned, got a good look at the driver. *Gotcha*

John Hammond and Riley arrived at the parking area at the Beaver Dam Reservoir before forensics. They would have missed the turn altogether except for the Loudon County Sheriff's cars with flashing blue lights. The deputies had put tape across the single lane, dirt turnoff. It cut away from the blacktop at a right angle between some trees and undergrowth. Riley and Hammond were saved from getting rear-ended as they quickly slowed for the turn because their unmarked cruiser was still recognizable as a police vehicle. The late model, full-sized sedan had black-wall tires, lots of antennas and one color of paint. People kept their distance.

Now, in the dirt circle near the reservoir, Riley and Hammond spoke to a Loudon County deputy.

"The bodies are down this path, not far. This is the fisherman who found them. Well, his dog found them. You want to talk to him first?"

"Yeah," Riley said. "You got his contact info?"

"Yeah, right here," the deputy replied.

He tore a page out of his notebook and handed it to Riley while Hammond stepped over to the Asian man with the fishing equipment.

"Your dog friendly?" Hammond asked.

The large husky remained by his owner. The eyes, one blue, one brown, made the dog look demonic, but the lolling tongue and slow wagging tail contradicted first impressions.

"He's okay," James Yung said.

He spoke in perfect English without any hint of an accent.

"His name is Ufu. My nephew named him. It was the first word out his mouth when he saw the dog."

"Hey Ufu," Hammond said to the dog.

Ufu appeared to smile.

"And you are?" Hammond said, looking up from the dog.

"James, James Yung," the man replied. "I just came down here to fish. School's out and I work nights, you know, waiter at Brennigan's? I used to fish here a lot when I was a kid."

"So you and Ufu found something?"

"Ufu did. I couldn't believe it. He wouldn't come when I called him, and when I went to see what he was doing I found him digging up a body. I made him stop, and I was just standing there looking and he started digging up another one. I called the police. Met them out by the road so they would know where to turn. I couldn't believe it."

"All right, James. We got your contact information from the deputy. We'll be in touch with you if we need you."

"Okay. Should I leave? Is it okay to go?" James asked.

"Yeah, you can go. Thanks for your time."

Hammond jotted a few notes, and rejoined Riley and the deputy.

"Ready to take a look?" Riley asked.

"Yeah, let's go."

The two followed the Deputy to the trail leading off into the woods. They traipsed down the path, a two-rut service path for official vehicles.

A chain across the entrance kept the traffic down to those who had a key for the padlock, mostly county workers emptying the trash drums by the water. Hammond and Riley both noticed the mishmash of footprints in the moist, Virginia clay, including Ufu's, and figured it a wash for forensics. Maybe things would be better at the burial sites.

They left the service road, turning into the woods on their left, and walked over the musty, Virginia forest floor a few yards to the first corpse. Eddie Spechi lay there disturbed by the dog and the deputies. The lifeless body oozed fluids and attracted bugs. The lack of decomposition said it hadn't been there long.

"Looks like a loser," Riley said. "Too skinny, crappy clothes; who would want to do him, you know? What for?"

Hammond studied the scene.

"Where's the other one?" he asked the deputy. "There's just one more, right?"

"Over this way. We have dogs on the way. So far, it's just the two."

Hammond and Riley stepped over to where the other body lay, partially uncovered. Ufu had uncovered an arm, a face and part of a torso, before James had stopped him.

"Looks like an old guy," Riley commented.

Three more deputies with two canines, tramped through the woods and the dogs began their search. Forensics from the state finally arrived and gleaned little from the surrounding area. There had been too much traffic. They went to work on the bodies and knew they had plenty to use for identification purposes: teeth, blood, hair and fingerprints. Hammond and Riley left them to their charge and went back to the station to do paperwork and drink coffee.

Chapter 18

"Come, my brother," Julia urged. "Take me to El Mercado and I will buy something for dinner. I will even cook when we get back."

They sat comfortably on the balcony of their apartment, and Angel didn't want to leave.

"Uhhm, I can't drive, I have been drinking," Angel complained.

"Oh, so you probably aren't hungry then," Julia replied. "I'll just have some popcorn. That will be enough for me for tonight."

"Uhhm, I think I can probably drive," Angel responded.

Julia's cooking was not to be passed up, ever.

Race fell in line two cars behind Sandi's Porsche. She couldn't possibly see his face, nor would she recognize the rental he drove. He followed her to the traffic light on Lee Highway. When the light turned green, the old Chevrolet in front of her turned left. So did Sandi and one of the cars separating her from Race. The other car between them went straight through the intersection.

Good, Race thought, and followed. *Still got one car between us.*

They pulled out onto Lee Highway in Fairfax near the old high school, where the road was four lanes wide with a center turn lane, straight, flat and bordered by every kind of fast food restaurant in existence. An abundance of gas stations and motels sprinkled both sides of the artery, and dozens of shops offered everything from cowboy boots to Mercury Zephyrs.

Sandi followed the old Chevrolet in front of her into a Latino market. Race drove by and turned at the next entrance to the large parking lot. He parked just beyond the grocery store where the parking lot formed a vertex for Lee Highway and Warwick Avenue. Lee Highway ran in front of the grocery, and Warwick Avenue ran behind it. Sandi had parked closer to the entrance at the far end of the store.

Race watched her climb out of the Porsche.

I'll grab her when she comes out, he told himself.

But she didn't walk directly to the store. She moved away from the entrance to where a man was getting out of the Chevrolet that had been in front of her.

"C'mon," Race heard her say. "Let's get what we need and get back to your place. I'm starving."

And she took his arm and pulled him toward the front door. She looked happy. The man looked mislead and not quite sure what to do about it. Race's brain simmered in the blood that rushed to his head.

I'll kill her. I'll just kill her and walk out. They won't catch me. Nobody knows me, and she deserves it.

He opened the glove box where he put the revolver and made sure it was loaded.

I don't care who else has to go down, he muttered.

The errant couple entered the market, him smiling with a puzzled look and her laughing. Race opened the car door, stood and pushed the pistol into his waistband. He walked toward the store as if drawn by some invisible force.

He walked in and saw Sandi and the man she had dragged in with her rounding the corner of the farthest aisle to the right. They pushed a shopping cart and looked too happy for Race. He moved quickly. He had no second thoughts. He rounded the corner and walked down the aisle unnoticed. Without missing a step, the pistol came out of his waistband. He walked up behind the couple, and his arm rose and fell. Jack crumpled to the floor, pulling the cart over with him. It sounded like a car wreck.

Jack made an attempt at jumping back up, as if to prove he wasn't hurt, but he couldn't. He wanted to lay there and die, and his body agreed.

He rolled over and saw Race holding a pistol straight out, pointing at Sandi, then at him, then back at Sandi.

It's him, Jack thought. *I'm going to die anyway, why not just lie here?*

But he couldn't, and he knew it. Had his mother had taught him all about honor, or was it his father who taught him? Either way, he knew he had to stand in harms way to protect another. It was his duty, the right thing to do. More than likely nothing he could do would help. He would just stand there and take a bullet, and they would die anyway, but he had to stand.

A store manager ran around the corner to investigate the racket and stopped so fast he nearly fell. A woman screamed at the other end of the aisle, turned her basket around and fled.

Like a man made of heavy clay, Jack struggled to his feet while the acute throbbing in his head expanded and contracted with every accelerated heartbeat. His lumbar muscles tightened spastically causing him to arch his back. His right hand went to the back of his head and came back sticky and red.

Sandi had backed up against the vegetable cooler, and before Jack could move between her and the weapon pointed at her face, she lost control of her bladder. She slid to the floor and sat in her own puddle.

In his struggle to rise, Jack hadn't noticed her go down. His feet dragged him to a spot in between her and Race. Facing the pistol that would likely take his life, he did not look or feel like a hero. His right hand had returned to the back of his head, and his left hand now reached toward his twisted and curved back. Would he die doing a bad version of the Macarena?

But he stood. Not because he wanted to, and not because he was courageous or chivalrous. He stood because he was supposed to. He would die doing something right. As the inevitability sunk in, he became more curious than afraid. A painful calm enveloped him, and he almost wished for the bullet. There was nothing else to do but stand.

How is this going to go down? he wondered, but it didn't matter. He was a goner.

Chapter 19

The fleeing woman nearly ran over Angel and Julia with her grocery cart.

She kept screaming, "Oh, my God, Oh, my God!"

Angel's professional instincts usurped his survivor instincts and he ran toward the source of her panic instead of away from it. Julia followed, wanting to protect Angel.

Angel peeked around the corner from behind the rack of sale-priced chips and dip on the end cap. He reached for his weapon and came up empty. He wore shorts and a T-shirt, but no holster.

Damn the heat! I should be armed, Angel thought.

Julia ran up behind Angel and looked over his shoulder. She saw Jack, standing between certain death and a frightened, crying shopper. Her guts threatened to tear her apart. She had to stop whatever would happen.

Race squeezed the trigger just as 100 pounds of something hit him in the ribs. He spun as he fell, and his shot sent a bullet through the ceiling near Angel. Angel charged. He had been too slow to stop Julia, but he would not forsake her. Jack's eyes slammed shut with the shot, and he stood awaiting the unknowable. It never arrived. He opened his eyes to see Julia entangled with the gunman on the floor. He lurched forward just as Angel grabbed Julia. Jack fell on Race long enough for Angel to disengage his sister from the melee. Race brought the pistol down hard on Jack's head for the second time in as many minutes. He wriggled out from under Jack's limp frame, holding Angel at bay with the .357. Angel held Julia behind him and stared hard at Race.

"This isn't over!" Race railed.

His eyes never left Angel, but he directed his rage toward Sandi, who continued to melt into tears and urine.

Julia wriggled and broke free of her brother's hold. She was immediately at Jack's side as he moaned and tried once again to rise above his circumstances. For the second time he found himself unable.

"Jack! Jack!" Julia cried as she rolled him to his side.

Race glanced at them but kept his weapon leveled on Angel.

"I'm okay," he whispered, dazed. "Julia?"

"Jack," she breathed and pulled him closer; a tear ran down her cheek and into his hair.

Race backed up toward the head of the aisle where the terrified store manager took two steps back and bumped the apple bin, knocking a few loose. Race turned quickly at the sound, and just as quickly, Angel was on him.

Race fought viciously, but, with the element of surprise on his side, Angel would not be defeated. Using his strength and training, he disarmed Race and the brutal skirmish ended with Angel's knee in Race's back, and Race's own weapon pointed at the back of his head.

"This isn't over," he threatened again, grunting under the strain, his mouth turned to one side to avoid licking the floor.

One of the guys who stocked produce had dialed 911, and the City of Fairfax police arrived. It seemed to have taken hours, but in fact they appeared in less than five minutes. They arrested Race, and called for two ambulances: one for Jack, who was bleeding, and one for Sandi, who was hysterical. Eventually the parking lot lit up with emergency vehicles: several cruisers, two ambulances, and even a fire truck. It blocked the shopper's cars for quite some time before finally turning off its flashing lights and pulling slowly away.

Inside, officers tried to control the situation and find out what had happened. Two paramedics took Sandi out on a stretcher while two others attended to Jack. They separated Julia from him, questioned him about pain, and asked how many fingers they were holding up while they talked to a doctor via radio.

"Don't ever do that again." Angel scolded, holding Julia in his arms.

Julia let Angel hold her close, but she never took her eyes off Jack. Tears ran down her cheeks.

"Help me to understand, okay? Just be patient. When you say 'Race,' you mean Mr. Hardin. Is that correct? That's what you told us at the house, right?" Hammond coaxed Sandi.

The Valium began to produce the desired result and Sandi's speech improved.

"Yes," she answered, hugging the hospital gown and pulling on the sheet and blanket. "Yes, he tried to kill me."

"And you think it was because he saw you and Mr. Casey together?"

"Yes, yes, he saw us. He's crazy! You've got to help me!"

Riley looked more puzzled than concerned, but Hammond assured Sandi that she would be protected. They rose to leave.

"Mr. Hardin has been arrested, and there's an officer right outside your door, okay? Nobody can come in unless he lets them."

One of the City police detectives had called Hammond when they found one of the missing persons: John Racine Hardin. Now Hammond and Riley were trying to make sense of the situation. Outside Sandi's hospital room they shared thoughts.

"I don't like it," Riley said. "'He saw us' she says, but what was he doing there? Nobody has seen him since yesterday morning and he shows up at a grocery store two blocks from his house? Is he stalking Ms. Anderson? I don't like it, John."

Hammond looked at him. He knew when Riley called him 'John' that he was serious.

"I believe your sense about the whole thing is right on. Something stinks," Hammond said.

Riley looked back at Hammond. He knew when Hammond said 'something stinks,' he meant it.

"Let's see if Mr. Casey has anything to add, unless of course he wants to continue keeping secrets," Riley said.

"He is a little less than forthcoming, isn't he?"

Jack sat up in bed. The doctors at Fair Oaks Hospital wanted to keep him overnight because of his head injuries. Jack wanted out. He suffered from a mild concussion and a laceration that required twelve stitches to close. The combination gave him a headache that felt terminal. He thought about people who suffer from migraines.

How do they keep their sanity, he wondered.

He couldn't remember how it felt to be healthy, but he knew he wanted the feeling back.

"Mr. Casey, are you up to a visit?" a nurse peaked through the door.

"Yeah," Jack massaged his neck. "I guess so."

Julia? he hoped.

Jack's spirit sank back to the depths of self-pity as he watched Hammond and Riley walk through the door.

"Mr. Casey? You okay?" Riley took a few cautious steps.

"I guess," Jack answered.

"Sorry to disturb you," Riley apologized, "but we need some answers."

He and John Hammond walked in and a slightly callous attitude stole in behind them. Riley walked around the end of the bed and stood by the window. Hammond assumed a position near the door. If Jack didn't have a splitting headache before, he did now.

"You have a real knack for popping up in the middle of our investigations, Jack. Can I call you Jack? You're starting to become pretty familiar."

"Yeah, you can call me 'Jack'." Jack's answer sounded like an exasperated moan. "Look, I just met Sandi. I knew who she was but we had never really spoken. And that guy, I wouldn't have even recognized him. I just figured by the situation…"

"So you've never seen him before," Riley's inflection made the statement an insinuation, not a question.

He took out his notebook and a pen and acted as if he were noting the fact.

Hammond's presence in Jack's peripheral vision unnerved him.

"No! I've seen him before, just not often enough to recognize him. I mean, we never had anything to do with each other. Occasionally, on a Saturday, I would see him. You know, because I work Saturdays and he doesn't. So I would see him at his house. Er, Sandi's house." Jack paused and added, "...where they lived."

"So you knew him," Riley affirmed.

He acted as if he had finished documenting the information.

"No! I've seen him before, that's all. Maybe a few times, but out on my route. I see a lot of people. I don't always think much of it, or recognize them when I see them somewhere else, you know? Like at a grocery store, I'll see someone that I recognize, but I don't know where I know them from."

"So you do know him."

"No."

"But you recognized Sandi at the 7—11," Hammond interrupted, but it seemed a ploy, like something he and Riley rehearsed.

They had Jack off balance. It was a great way to get someone to blurt out the truth.

"Okay, Mr. Casey, tell us why this man attacked you."

"I guess because I was with his girlfriend, but she seemed scared before that, I mean before I met her, er, ran into her at the 7—11. You heard her. At her house, you interviewed her," Jack ran over himself by way of explanation.

"We know what Ms. Anderson said, Mr. Casey. But you don't know why he attacked you other than shopping with his roommate at the grocery store?" Hammond sounded as accusatory as Riley had.

Jack thought, *This is great Bad cop, bad cop.*

"He's got a point," Hammond said after he and Riley left Jack's room.

Their footsteps on the tile, a dinner cart and some rolling gurneys blended with his words to form a cacophonic tap dance in the hallway.

"What do you mean?" Riley asked, his words ricocheting hard off the walls.

"She was afraid before she ever got caught with Casey," Hammond replied.

Chapter 20

"She knows he killed his mother," Riley offered.

He and Hammond were walking towards their government-owned vehicle in the parking lot. The asphalt radiated hot air and an occasional tar bubble burst under their shoes. The pavement smelled new as it simmered.

"But the mother's been dead for months. How come he wants to kill his girlfriend now?" Hammond asked.

"She just found out," Riley countered.

"How come he killed the two guys he rides to work with?" Hammond continued.

"They just found out, too," Riley offered without thinking.

"How? He started bragging? Or she found the old woman and he confessed? Or she guessed? And what? Told the two riders? I don't like it. Start over."

"Casey killed Hardin's mother and stole his girlfriend…"

"No way. Hardin was after her before that, at least according to Angel Iglesias. And Iglesias is good. I don't think he was mistaken about that," Hammond said.

He unlocked the sedan and opened the door. It felt like opening a car-sized pizza oven. Riley opened the other door and stepped back.

"Geez…unbelievable."

Both men stepped back to let convection alleviate some of the heat.

"Start the car! Put the air on!" Riley insisted.

Hammond was already in motion. Both men's shirts dampened during their short wait for a cooler temperature. The 104° F in the parking lot was the coolest so far. After a minute, they crossed the threshold of the automobile and shut the doors. It hadn't cooled as fast as they would have liked, but it was better.

"Ouch!" Hammond jerked his hands away from the steering wheel.

"Okay, Casey didn't do it," Riley said, ignoring his partner's distress. "He's the mailman on that route, and he really did just happen to run into the Andersen woman at the 7-11. So what's going on?"

"The 'George and Eddy' guys killed Race's mother so he killed them," Hammond offered.

"And he found out she was dead months later? And they killed her so that...what? Nah, Hardin killed her."

John Hammond pulled out his handkerchief to cover the steering wheel so he could touch it.

Echols could hardly endure knowing his client possessed a ticket worth $11 million. He sat in his downstairs office with a drink in his hand. He didn't know the ticket sat in police custody with the rest of John Racine Hardin's possessions.

This is insane, he told himself, *and tomorrow the insanity ends.*

The lottery commission was expecting him. He would exchange the ticket for a receipt.

And it will drive me crazy until I get the check, he thought. *And the check...Shall I have them make it to me? Then I can make a check to Hardin. Of course, they'll take out taxes, and I'll take out my fee. Just to get a day's interest...any part of $11 million is going to be huge. I can make a thousand dollars a day for as long as I can stall him.*

The evil in Race Hardin didn't seem as formidable in his absence. Echols decided he would have his own name put on the check.

"Cripes!" the phone rang and nearly caused an out of body experience.

Echols sloshed a little of his third, and certainly not last, glass of scotch as he leaned forward to answer the phone.

"Echols," he burped, dispensing with formality. It was after hours.

"Get down here, now," a quiet voice commanded. "I'm in jail."

"Who...?" Echols fumbled for words.

"Race Hardin. You're my attorney. Now, get down here. I'm in the Fairfax County jail."

"What the hell...?"

"Now."

Race said it with authority and just a hint of a threat. The line went dead.

Chapter 21

Wednesday morning separate doctors at Fair Oaks hospital deemed Jack, and then Sandi, well enough to finish recovering on their own. One of the hospital volunteers called a cab for Jack, and, as he waited in the mandatory wheelchair, Sandi exited the elevator. She, too, sat in a wheelchair; a nurse pushed her into the lobby.

"Over there," she told the nurse as she pointed at Jack. Then she called, "Jack!"

She tried to push the wheels of her chair, but the young professional behind her said, "Whoa, girl. You need to sit right here. I'll take you where you need to go."

Sandi sat as ordered, and the nurse pushed her through a flurry of patients and visitors to where Jack waited.

"Is this where you want to be, with this handsome young man? I can see why." She gave Jack a wink and he grinned then winced.

"I don't look that bad, do I?" the robust woman asked.

"No, no, not at all," Jack flushed. "It just hurts to smile," he said and smiled despite himself. He winced again.

"Now, are you okay here?" she said to Sandi. "Do you still need that cab?"

"I've got one coming," Jack offered. "We can share," and then thought, *Damn! What did I say that for?*

"Thank you," Sandi murmured.

"Okay, then, I'll leave you two here for now." Sandi's nurse moved away.

"Are you okay? I was terrified. He's crazy." Sandi grabbed Jack's arm.

"Yeah, I'll live."

"Can I still stay with you? I'm afraid to go home," Sandi blurted. She spoke rapidly, barely keeping her mouth and her mind in sync.

"Uh, yeah, sure, I guess," Jack stammered. He would rather have been alone, or, better still, with Julia.

Race's arraignment hadn't gone well, but the bad news wasn't unexpected. The charges against him were stalking, assault, and attempted murder. Other charges would be brought as soon as the District Attorney had a chance to look over the crime report. There would be no bail. The accused was a flight risk and a threat to society. Now, Race sat in a holding cell in the jail attached to the back of the Fairfax County, high-rise courthouse. Echols sat across the table from him.

"These things take time," Echols whined.

Carefully pronouncing each word, Race replied, "I don't care." Continuing in a conversational tone, he reiterated his idea: "Offer the judge $1,000,000 to set bail. When I get out, he gets paid."

"I know, I know," Echols continued whining, "but I have to be careful. I could end up in here with you." As an afterthought he added, "Then where would we be?"

"Just do it," Race glared at the nervous counselor. Echols couldn't return his look.

Julia used her ten-minute break to call Fair Oaks Hospital. "He was in room 304," she told the operator. After a moment she asked, "Are you sure? I think he was badly hurt." Finally she added, "Alright. Thank you." She hung up. *He must be at home,* she thought. *I'll go to see him after work. Oh, my poor Jack.*

"It's the same caliber," Riley spoke as he hung up the phone.

Hammond bit his lower lip. "I'm not surprised. We'll know for sure when they finish in ballistics. I think he did it to cover his tracks."

They were checking Race's pistol against the slug found lodged in the brain of the unfortunate motel clerk.

"Okay," Riley began. "He kills his carpool, drives to his mother's house to ditch the truck, picks up her car, and...where's her car?"

"Loudon County found it at the airport where he got the rental. He left his mother's Lumina in long term parking," Hammond answered, and added, "and why did he kill his carpool?"

"And who killed his mother?" Riley countered.

"And why was he stalking Anderson?" the reciprocity continued.

The two detectives stared at each other. Finally, Riley moved, rubbing his temples and closing his eyes.

"Motives, we need motives." The words escaped him through clenched teeth.

"Casey and Anderson are having an affair," Hammond offered.

Riley opened his eyes. "Yeah, Casey. He's the wildcard in all of this. He goes to the house everyday."

"And money."

"And money, what?" Riley asked, looking at Hammond like a sugar-crazed leprechaun.

"That's another good motive," Hammond answered, as if Riley hadn't spoken at all.

"There is no money, John," Riley got serious.

Hammond drummed his fingers on his desktop and stared at Riley. After a few moments, his fingers stopped abruptly.

"Sure there is, Einstein," he said and smiled at his partner.

It was Riley's turn to stare. All at once, the Rubik's cube in his mind lined up.

"Right! Einstein. The social security check. Delivered by Casey..."

"...to Anderson..."

"...who killed the mother..."

"Who killed the mother?" Hammond asked, and not without some skepticism.

"Who indeed," Riley retracted his conclusion.

"We need to go to the bank; see who's been cashing those checks."

Jack and Sandi sat in the backseat of the cab. Sandi sat touching Jack with her right arm looped behind his left and her hand in his. Their fingers were intertwined.

She must really be shaken, Jack thought. "Are you okay?" he asked.

"I'm really frightened. Why did Race kill George and Eddie? What's going to happen now? I don't know what to do," Sandi babbled. "He's a murderer! His mother, his friends, even that girl at the motel! I'm so glad they caught him."

The cabby sneaked a surprised and intrigued look in the rearview mirror. He had carried some interesting passengers, but none that had direct contact with killers.

"So am I," Jack said. "My head can't take much more of him. Let's just get my car and go home. Uh, both cars. Can you drive?"

"I don't know. Can we just pick up the Porsche? You can drive, and we can pick up your car tomorrow. You're not going to work tomorrow, are you? I'm not. I can't."

"No, I'm, uh, off for the...for a...for tomorrow. Maybe we can get you situated then."

Jack didn't want to encourage anything, and he didn't trust his own instincts. He didn't trust Sandi either.

I wish she'd let go of my hand. Does she think we're something? Whatever the situation, Jack felt uncomfortable. *I don't like it. Where's Julia when I need her?*

Sandi snuggled closer. "Thank you, Jack," she whispered.

They rode in silence the rest of the way to the market where they had parked the evening before. The cab driver pulled up to the curb as close to the door as possible. Jack gave him a twenty, all he had, and told him to keep the change. Sandi searched her purse for the keys to the Porsche.

"Here they are," she said, and handed them to Jack. "I parked over here."

She tugged at Jack who began to follow when someone shouted, "Hey!"

Jack and Sandi stopped abruptly and turned toward the voice. A man in a short sleeved, white shirt and a red and blue tie walked rapidly from the store toward them.

"I saw you get out of the cab. I'm the assistant manager, remember? I was at the end of the aisle. Are you two okay?"

"Yeah, we'll live," Jack answered.

"I couldn't believe that guy, attacking you like that. Why'd he do that? The cops wouldn't tell me anything."

Jack looked at Sandi. She gave him a passive look, permission to speak for both of them. It made them seem more like a couple, and like maybe that was the reason for the attack.

Jack looked back at the eager questioner. "He's got problems, you know, big problems." Then he closed the subject with, "Are you okay? That was a pretty close call, with that gun and everything."

"Yeah, I'm okay," the assistant manager answered.

His disappointment at the evasive answer caused his shoulders to slump, and he diverted his eyes. He was pretty sure he knew what was going on.

These two made a fool of that guy who attacked them. He's a cheated on husband or lover or something. I'd have attacked them, too. I hope he gets out and goes after them again.

"Hey, can I leave my car here one more night?" Jack asked. "It's that Chevy over there; I can move it to the back of the lot if you want. We just can't both drive right now, you know?"

"Oh. Yeah. Just move it back a row or two. I'll tell my boss it's here, and that you'll pick it up tomorrow," he muttered....*too laid back, always gettin' walked on.*

Jack moved his car and he and Sandi took off in the Porshce.

Chapter 22

Hammond and Riley looked at the copies of the social security checks, all signed by John R. Hardin. They also looked at the power of attorney the bank had on file while they sat in the branch manager's office. The manager sat behind his desk, his manicured hands clasped in front of him. A very young and timid woman stood near the door, and Hammond and Riley turned toward her.

"But you say Monday a man cashed the check, only every other time it's a woman?" Riley spoke to the woman, trying to be gentle.

The woman, or girl, really, replied, "Yes, that's right. Usually, a woman deposits it in her checking account, but this time a guy cashed it."

"It was Mr. Hardin," the manager offered. "I was here when he filed the power of attorney with us, though I wouldn't have recognized him right away. But we, Theresa and I," he said, nodding toward the young teller, "checked his ID. It was him alright."

"And the woman who usually deposits it?" Riley asked. "What was up with that?"

"We checked that situation thoroughly," the manager nearly leapt from his chair. He wanted to protect his bank's reputation as well as his own. "When Mr. Hardin started banking here, he said sometimes a Ms....uh," he fumbled with some papers on his desk.

"Anderson," his teller supplied the name. "Sandra Anderson."

"Yes, he said sometimes Ms. Anderson would bring the check in. Lately it's been most of the time," he settled back into his chair feeling vindicated. "He said the check belonged to his invalid mother, and that they both took care of her."

"Can I get a copy of records showing all the times she deposited that check?" Riley asked.

"Certainly," the manager told him. "May I send Ms. Chase back to the window now?"

"Yeah, Yeah," Riley seemed always happy to comply. "And thank you, Ms. Chase. Uh, we may need you again. We'll call on you here if we do."

Outside, Hammond looked at Riley over the roof of their unmarked car.

"C'mon, start the car, get it cooled off," Riley complained.

"I want to see how long Ms. Anderson's been depositing that check compared with how long Thelma Hardin's been dead," Hammond answered as he unlocked the car.

Both men opened their doors and involuntarily took a step back.

"Geez!" Riley continued to complain.

"I think that's what you said the last time," Hammond observed.

Then he got half way in, started the car and the air conditioner, and got back out.

"Were she and Hardin partners in this scam, or was she doing her own thing?" Hammond wanted to know.

"No, she and Casey were in cahoots," Riley said. "Casey's in this up to his neck."

"Probably," Hammond thought out loud. "Probably."

They both got in the car.

"Ouch "

Hammond put his handkerchief over the steering wheel.

Echols left Race Hardin in the Fairfax County Jail. He couldn't shake the image of the look Hardin had given him.

'Just do it,' he says. And how am I supposed to 'do it'?

Echols lumbered through the halls of justice on his way to the Circuit Court Judges Chambers. His fellow pedestrians ran the gamut of low life to high class, and Echols fell somewhere below the mid-range.

Successful attorneys hurried by. The one's working in tandem conversed in language as crisp as their images. Echols, on the other hand, wore a disheveled suit and his tie hung loosely about his neck beneath both of his chins.

But he had luck on his side today: Circuit Court Judge Norwich Deaber had just recessed for lunch.

"Your honor!" he called out as Deaber hurried toward his chambers.

Judge Deaber looked back without slowing down.

"What can I do for you counselor?"

Echols followed him into the office.

"Well?"

"Can I speak to you briefly? It's about the Hardin case."

"How briefly, counselor? I'd like to get some lunch." The judge sat behind his desk and allowed himself to relax; you could almost see his robes wrinkle.

"Very briefly," Echols said and closed the door behind him.

"Sit," his honor surrendered to the interruption.

"Your honor, my client needs to be out of jail. He could make bail if you set it, even if you set it for a lot. Um, he would be very grateful. To you, personally, and, um, he can afford to be grateful, if, you know…" Echols spoke stiltingly.

"Meaning…?" the judge was abrupt.

"Well, he's a generous man. He enjoys sharing."

Judge Deaber leaned forward, his forearms mashing the piles of paper on his desk. "Are you talking about your client paying a judge to throw a trial?"

"No, no, no, your honor," Echols rapidity nearly caused him to trip on his tongue. "He just wants bail, nothing that would look like you were doing him any favors, your honor. Set it high; that would be reasonable."

Deaber thought of his ex-wife and the thrashing she had recently given him in court and at the bank.

I live like a pauper, while she runs around with rich attorneys, and lives on my money; in my house; driving my car; just because she caught me with someone one time! She was a prostitute, for chrissake, she used sex whenever she could to get out of being arrested. What could possibly be wrong with doing someone a little favor in exchange for a light sentence?

But this guy, Hardin, even if he can afford the deposit on a million dollar bail, how much is he going to have left?

Echols bowels were loose. He could be on his way to jail with his client.

"How generous could your client possibly be after $100,000 to a bail bondsman?" Deaber asked.

Echols felt physical relief at the judge's interest in the proposal.

"He could pay the bondsman the 10% and give the other 90% to someone who helped him out," Echols volunteered. Hardin had said to offer the judge a $1,000,000. *That also leaves $100,000 for me,* he thought gleefully. It had been a spur of the moment idea,...*and it just might work.*

"He doesn't look like he can afford a pot to piss in," the judge commented, leaning back.

"I assure you, he has the means to be very generous. He's a benevolent man. I have a copy here," Echols leaned to pick up his briefcase, "of a lottery ticket. Please, hear me out. You may have heard that there is a winner of the state lottery jackpot. Hardin has the winning ticket, or more specifically, the Fairfax County Police have it with his personal belongings. I can cash it for him, post his bail and, well…" he let the words hang. "But he needs someone to authorize his release, if you know what I mean."

Judge Deaber looked at the copy of the lottery ticket and tossed it back to Echols. Then he folded his hands under his chin and, looking straight through Echols, he thought. Finally, he said, "When I have $900,000, I will release Mr. Hardin on $1,000,000 bail. I will see to it that you have access to his personal belongings, which I assume are negligible, other than the lottery ticket. And no one knows it has any value, is that correct?"

"Yessir," Echols rushed to answer, "Yessir, that's right. I can have the money, uh, tomorrow? I think I can, anyway."

"Now if that's all," Deaber said, "I need something to eat. I'll see you tomorrow, counselor."

Chapter 23

Jack drove the Porsche to his house without testing its legendary engineering.

I just want to go to bed, he thought. *I don't think I need a house guest right now, not even an attractive woman.*

He had to laugh at himself for wishing someone like Sandi would just go away.

I must be getting old, or that bump on the head did more damage than I thought.

Hammond and Riley arrived at the jail about the same time as Echols, who had just returned from speaking to the judge.

"We're here to see one John Racine Hardin," Riley said to the officer behind the bullet proof glass. He flashed his shield as he spoke.

Echols stopped short behind Hammond and Riley, looking guilty, though he needn't have; no one paid any attention to him.

"Step inside, please," the window man said as he pushed a buzzer to let the detectives in.

Riley pulled the door open, and heard a voice behind him.

"Uh, I'm his attorney," Echols announced.

Hammond, Riley and the uniformed officer in charge of the entry all stopped and looked at him.

"Whose attorney?" the officer asked.

"John Hardin's. I'd like to be present when they question him," Echols said.

Echols handled mostly divorces and bankruptcies. Pronouncing himself counsel for the defense in a serious criminal matter unnerved him.

"The door's open, sir," the uniform said to Riley.

"Oh, sorry," Riley said, and walked in with Hammond right behind him.

Hammond let the door go in Echols face.

"Can I see some ID?" the guard spoke to Echols.

"Yeah, I was just here," Echols said, fumbling for his wallet.

"Gotta see it, every time," the guard said.

Echols slid his driver's license under the window and the guard checked it, and logged it in. Hammond and Riley stood and waited.

Jack helped Sandi carry her overnight bag in.

"Hey, Bug " he said as the little dog met them at the door.

Bug wagged and rubbed against Jack's legs like he couldn't get close enough. Then he noticed Sandi and became cautious.

"Hi," Sandi said with a hint of disdain and held out her hand.

The offering seemed insincere and Bug backed up with a snarl.

"Hey," Jack said. Then to Sandi, "He's just hungry and has to go out is all. He doesn't usually act like this." *That's weird,* he thought.

Jack put Bug and some food out on the back patio and returned his attention to Sandi.

"Make yourself at home. It's not much," he said, "but it's comfortable."

They walked directly into the living room/dining room/kitchen of Jack's little rambler. A hallway to the right led to three bedrooms and a bath. The master bedroom had a bathroom of its own.

"This is nice, Jack," Sandi said, and not entirely as an afterthought, added, "And so are you." She turned to face him. "I don't know what I would do without your help."

"Um, it's no big deal," Jack stammered. "I mean, anybody would've."

"No, not just anybody," Sandi whispered. "You stood up to an armed man, for me."

She took his chin in her hand and turned his face toward hers and kissed him, slowly. Then they looked at each other from millimeters apart.

"I, uh, you can sleep, um, down here," Jack finally broke the spell. He picked up her bag and headed down the hallway. "Here's the bathroom," he said pointing as he walked by, "and this room is a mess. It's my office. And, well, there's all kinds of junk in there. But, here's my extra bedroom. It's ready for use, I think; might be a little dusty."

Sandi followed him into the small bedroom. It had a double bed, a dresser, a nightstand, and flowered curtains on the window. They matched the spread on the bed.

"My ex-wife," he remembered this time that he and she had split, "did all the furnishing. I left it the way she left...well, you know; it looks better than anything I could've done."

He put Sandi's bag on the bed.

"It really is nice," Sandi said from behind him, and gently took his hand.

"I, uh, I'll be right across the hall here," Jack said without looking at her. "I think I need to take another pain-killer. Make yourself at home. I'll be right back."

He tried to smile without wincing as he turned to leave.

Race and Echols cast furtive glances at each other from across the table. Riley sat next to Echols and put a notebook and pencil on the table. Hammond stood, leaning on the wall by the door behind Echols. From his vantagepoint he could stare at Hardin, keep him off balance, and make Echols nervous just by being behind him.

"You threatened a woman with her life; pistol whipped her boyfriend and assaulted a police officer while resisting arrest. You're going to do time, Hardin; that's a given," Riley gave no quarter. "How much time is still up to you. I want to know about two men we found in Loudon County; I want to know about your mother; and I want to know about a motel clerk near Front Royal," Riley fired the commands rapidly, leaving no response time in between. Then he stared hard at Race, as did Hammond.

"You don't have to say anything that will…" Echols sounded timid.

"Shut up!" Race looked directly at his attorney. Then, ignoring Hammond and Echols, he shifted his attention to Riley. "That bitch killed my mother!" he nearly shouted. "She killed her and took the money, killed my mother to pay for a damned sports car!" Hatred oozed from every pore in his body.

"Tell me about that," Riley relaxed and spoke calmly. "What was Anderson doing with your mother's social security check? We've been to the bank. We know she deposited the check into her account most of the time; but you signed it. What was going on?"

"I'll take care of it," Race seethed.

"No, you'll do time for killing your mother, unless you cooperate," Riley countered, still calm.

Race looked down momentarily, then back up at Riley. "My mother needed someone to take care of her. I did it until I met Sandi. When she saw how bad it was between us, between me and my mother," he almost hissed, "she offered to make sure the old woman was taken care of. I guess she did that alright."

"It sounds like you hated your mother," Riley said.

"I did. But, she was still my mother. I wasn't going to kill her!"

"What about Casey?" Riley asked.

"Who?"

"Casey, the mailman," Riley acted nonchalant.

"I'll kill him if I ever see him again," Race said.

"Hardin," Hammond's voice commanded attention.

Race looked at him for the first time since he entered the room. Echols turned around in his chair. Riley played with his pencil, still facing away from his partner.

"Threatening someone is against the law. You just did it in front of two police officers," Hammond said.

He appeared ready to continue when Riley cut him off. "Mr. Hardin, I can understand your emotional response, but we need your cooperation."

The hate filled eyes turned back to Riley. Echols turned back around.

"The two guys you rode to work with are dead; forensics can prove you killed them," Riley lied. "The girl at the motel is dead. I know you killed her. The bullet in her head came from your gun. And you say you hated your mother, but you didn't kill her? I don't know, Hardin."

"That bitch killed her!"

Race leapt to his feet. His chair clattered half way across the room behind him. Hammond rounded the table and stopped, towering over Race, who stood, wearing a blaze orange jump suit and shackled, hands and feet. Race turned his head toward Hammond. A smile tinged with insanity spread over his face. Riley had never flinched and remained seated, leaning back, relaxed. Echols's eyes grew big and he frantically pushed back from the table. The quick action caused his chair to tilt, and he scrambled from it as it clattered to the floor. He stood by the door, and his eyes darted from face to face, but no one looked back at him. It was as if he didn't exist.

A hundred hours seemed compressed into the moment, and then Riley said, "We'll get back to you on that."

He glanced at Hammond who caught the look, but kept his glare on Hardin. Hammond's glower said, 'give me a reason...' Hardin slowly turned his face toward Riley. He was still wearing his insane smile like a mask of insanity.

"Well, John," Riley said in a friendly manner, "what do you say we leave Mr. Hardin here with his attorney?"

He wore a little sadistic smile of his own as he picked up his pencil and notebook. John Hammond stared at Race Hardin up to the last possible second before turning toward the door. Ignoring Echols, he nearly knocked him over as he left the room.

Riley followed him, pausing just long enough to look back at the two disparate men. Still wearing a smile, he said, "Have a nice day."

Chapter 24

Hammond and Riley sat in their car and ate junk food from a fast food restaurant. They kept the motor running and the AC on.

"I don't know," Riley mused. "He killed three people for no apparent reason, but he wants us to think he didn't kill his mother even though he claims he hated her. Aw, shhi...." He dabbed at some ketchup on his shirt.

"He said something about a sports car. The Porsche, I'm guessing," Hammond chewed thoughtfully.

"You think she did it?"

"I think somebody helped her."

"Casey?"

"Let's go ask him. We'll get back to Hardin's motives later."

"Okay, but before we question Casey, let's go talk to his boss. Let's see what kind of stellar character we're dealing with."

Julia had started work at 5:30 AM, and by 2 PM she had had enough. *No overtime today*, she thought. *I'm tired and I'm leaving.*

She gathered her belongings and stopped at the ladies room before punching out.

This is a dirty job she told herself as she washed up.

Outside of the bathroom door she heard the voices of some men walking by. One voice belonged to Morey. The other two sounded familiar, but she couldn't quite place them.

"Come on in to my office," Morey was saying. "We can talk there. I'll show you his record. It's not great, I can tell you that."

The footsteps faded and Julia came out of bathroom. The time clock was attached to the wall to her right, but she cast a furtive glance to her left as she turned.

It's those detectives that Angel spoke to in the parking lot, she thought. *Talking to Morey? That could only be about Jack. I wonder why they investigate him. I should tell him. I should see him anyway; to visit the sick, which is part of life. Well, to visit the injured. I hope he is okay.*

Julia punched out and went to her car.

Now, where does Jack live?

She couldn't ask Morey; he was with the detectives.

He wouldn't tell me anyway, she thought. *I'll find someone who knows.*

Julia looked in every direction, but not many people were around when the carriers were on the street. She noticed Joe, the guy in charge of vehicle maintenance, walking toward his hole-in-the-wall office with reports in hand, telling him which truck needed what, and when it was due.

He will know! I hear Jack saying they fish together.

"Joe!" she called. "Excuse me. Can you help me, please?"

Joe stopped walking at the sound of his name, and turned toward the direction of the voice. He wore an exasperated look, having dealt with too many carriers who didn't check their vehicles when they were supposed to, and then, when it was time to go, had an 'emergency' flat tire that had to be fixed 'right now.' His look changed, however, when he saw Julia walking toward him. Joe was an unpretentious man and able to see the beauty without the veneer. Besides, she didn't drive a postal vehicle. Maybe she just needed help changing locks in the box section. They could be frustrating sometimes.

"Hi, Julia, what can I do for you?"

"I want to visit Jack," she blurted out, and her bronze face reddened. Sometimes, as she translated her thoughts to English, they came out less than tactful. "I mean he is hurt, so I want to visit him and be sure he is alright. But I don't know where he lives. Can you tell me? I know you and Jack are friends."

What a lucky guy, Joe thought. Then he said, "Yeah, I can help you. But, hey, do you want my address, in case I get injured?" and thought, *It might be worth it.*

Julia laughed. "No! You don't want to be injured. Besides, I can find your house from Jack."

"Well, okay, if you're sure you can find it. Anyway, Jack lives in Sterling Park. Do you know where that is? Out route 28? I don't have his address, I just know where he lives."

Joe gave Julia directions to Jack's house, written on the back of one of his reports. Julia thanked him and headed home to freshen up before she went visiting.

"He's been a problem since I've been here," Morey said.

Hammond and Riley sat opposite him in the Government Issue, gray metal chairs. At least they were cushioned.

"Late for work, lazy…" Morey continued his lies about Jack.

"What is he on suspension for anyway?"

"Insubordination; he acted in a threatening manner, too, in front of witnesses."

The story seemed to grow, from name calling to threatening, and from one witness to many. Morey enjoyed every minute of the interview.

"Do you know anything about his personal life? Does he have wife or a girlfriend?" Riley continued.

"Probably both," Morey sneered. "He's not what I would call the most reputable guy around."

"But you don't know for sure?"

"Well, I think I remember him taking time off to go to court. He was being divorced, so I guess maybe he doesn't have a wife anymore. Sometimes I see him hanging around that Mexican girl in the Box section, but I don't think she wants anything to do with him."

"What's her name? Is she here today?"

Outside, Hammond and Riley mulled over the latest information.

"No love lost there," Riley commented.

"Nope; no love lost there. I wonder if this Julia woman could give us a less biased assessment. Isn't she Trooper Iglesias' sister? Isn't he Peruvian? I wonder where that idiot got 'Mexican' from."

Riley laughed. Hammond didn't usually engage in character assassination, but his take on Morey seemed accurate.

"We'll have to catch her another time. Meanwhile, despite being an idiot, Mr. Stenich probably gave us a good description of Casey's moral code."

"Let's talk to Ms. Anderson about those checks, then to Casey again, just to rattle his cage."

But Sandi had left the hospital, and she wasn't at home.

"On to Casey's," Riley chronicled as he drove.

Chapter 25

"Why did Race kill those two other guys?" Jack asked. He and Sandi were sitting in his living room/dining room/kitchen. "And why is he after you?"

"He's crazy! He just snapped, I guess. He killed his mother, and now he's just killing everybody around him. I'm so glad they caught him. I hope he never gets out of jail."

Jack stood for a moment and then offered, "More coffee?"

"No, no, I'm fine."

"Well, excuse me for just a sec'. I think I'll get some." Jack was feeling a little better.

As he walked to the kitchen, he heard a knock on the door, and, before he could answer it, Sandi was on her feet.

"I'll get it," she called.

This woman is trying to take over my life! Jack thought.

Sandi swung the door open and stood, smiling her automatic, less than genuine, ticket agent smile at the two detectives, Hammond and Riley. At the same time Julia pull up to the curb in front of the house.

Why is she here? Julia wondered. *She's that girl from el Mercado. Is she visiting Jack?*

Hammond and Riley and Sandi looked at Julia, who looked back with uncertainty.

"Who is it?" Jack called, and walked up behind Sandi.

What now? he thought, eyeing the detectives. Then he spotted Julia. *Oh, no! Not now! This can't be happening now!*

Jack firmly moved Sandi aside and said, "Excuse me," as he parted the investigators.

"Hurry back, Honey," Sandi called behind him, more to catch Julia's attention than Jack's.

Jack ignored her and made a beeline to Julia, every step generating a stabbing sensation in the middle of his skull.

"Julia! Hi!"

"Maybe I should see you later, Jack. You have a lot of people here," Julia looked toward the front door of Jack's house.

Jack turned to look, also, and cringed at the sight: Sandi answering his door; calling him 'honey.' *Where did that come from?* He didn't care about the cops, but what would Julia think about Sandi being there?

He turned back to Julia and said, "No, please stay. These people are all...um, I don't know, but can you come in and wait? I'll see what they want."

"No, I think I better go," Julia said, turning her gaze back to Jack, who leaned on the top of her car as he looked in.

She's beautiful! Jack thought. *I've never seen anyone make shorts and flip-flops look so good. She's got to stay.*

"Please, Julia. I'd rather see you than any of those people."

"I don't think so, Jack." She sounded shy, but also wounded. "You better take care of your friend. I'll talk to you back at work. I just wanted to see if you were okay."

She pulled away from the curb, holding her hand up and curling her fingers down in a waving gesture that said, 'see ya.' Jack's heart broke.

Damn! Why now? Why did this have to happen now?

And as Julia left, she thought, *What a fool I am! He was just being nice to me, and I thought we could be together.* She told herself she was okay, but she wasn't. She hadn't noticed the depth of her feelings for Jack until now.

"Mind if we talk to the two of you?" Riley asked as Jack made an agonized walk back to the house. "I hope we're not interrupting anything."

Jack didn't like Riley's tone, or that Hammond and Riley were at his house, but he couldn't do anything about it. He didn't like Sandi being there either.

"No. I mean, no, you're not interrupting anything; we were just, um, having some coffee. What do you want?"

He didn't usually sound so blunt, but right now he didn't care.

"I kinda hoped you would invite us in. It's pretty hot out here, don't you think?"

"Oh, yeah. Come on in," Jack said as he pushed past everyone again.

"I thought I recognized the Porsche," Riley said, flashing a smile with just a hint of disdain.

"Sit down," Jack said, noting the disrespect in Riley's voice. "Coffee?"

I know, Mom, I'll be civil.

"No, thanks," Riley said and Hammond lowered his eyes, tightened his lips and shook his head.

"We just wanted to talk to both of you. We went to your house, Ms. Anderson," Riley looked toward where Sandi had taken a seat in a chair catty-cornered from the couch. "When we couldn't find you, we decided to talk to Mr. Casey here," he gestured toward Jack without looking at him, "and here you are! Must be our lucky day."

"I just need some company," Sandi almost whispered. "Jack has been kind enough to offer me a place to stay until my nerves settle."

And the sooner they do, the better, Jack thought, but he said nothing.

"Is that right, Mr. Casey? Good for you. You're a regular Good Samaritan," Riley sat on the couch and shifted his attention to Jack.

How long is this going to take? Jack wondered.

As if reading his mind, Hammond crossed the room and sat in the only other chair. He stared at Jack the whole time.

"Why don't you sit?" Riley patted the sofa cushion next to where he sat.

"I'm okay," Jack said, but he didn't sound okay, and he backed up five steps and dragged a chair from the dining area closer to the living area. The back of the chair faced the others and Jack straddled it, as if mounting a Shetland pony.

"Well, it's nice to see you both out of the hospital," Riley's social skills meandered.

An uncomfortable silence followed. Jack and Riley stared at each other, Riley smiling; Jack, not. Hammond sat with his elbows on the arms of the overstuffed chair he occupied. His hands were joined in front of his face with the index fingers forming a steeple that touched his lips. He looked like a statue, a variation of Auguste Rodin's 'The Thinker.' Sandi's frayed nerves couldn't take the silence.

"Who was that Mexican girl, Jack?" she asked, more to hear herself talk than anything else. Also, it kept the subject away from her and Race Hardin.

"She's Peruvian," Jack said.

"Oh, does she clean your house?" Sandi continued.

"No. She's my friend. At least I think she was. God only knows what she's thinking now," Jack looked right at Sandi.

"Oh. I didn't know. I mean, you're not dating her, are you?"

Riley laughed. "What would Angel think of that, John?" he said looking at his partner.

Hammond smirked and shook his head. He knew his partner was referring to Angel's thoughts about two things: his sister dating someone like Casey and the remarks of the pompous bigot sitting across the room.

Now, Jack had had enough. "Look, what do you guys want? I just need to get back to a little normalcy here. And who's Angel? Is he the dude in the Camaro?"

Hammond and Riley exchanged glances.

"Yeah," Riley said, smiling. "He's the dude in the Camaro."

Hammond finally spoke: "We're here because we don't know why Mr. Hardin killed all these people. We were hoping one of you might be able to provide us with some more information."

"You also might want to know," Riley interjected, "that he swears he did not kill his mother. That's kind of odd, considering he hasn't denied three other murders. He's going away for a long time."

"Why do you suppose he would deny only one out of four murders?" Hammond asked. He stared straight at Sandi.

"Don't you have enough evidence? He must have done it," she seemed near tears.

"I don't know," Riley said, keeping the conversation off balance. "Why would he? He said you did it."

With that bombshell, all eyes in the room were on Sandi. She sat, wringing her hands in the corner, trying to think of something to say other than, 'I didn't do it.'

"Yep, he said you did it for the money," Riley continued.

"There was no money!" Sandi cried.

"The people at your bank said you deposited her social security check every month," Hammond said.

"I did not!" Sandi screamed. She sounded like a little girl. "I mean," her voice became very soft, "I mean, he made me take it to the bank. I had to."

Jack stared in disbelief. *Who is this woman?*

"And, Mr. Casey," Riley turned his attention to Jack, "I suppose he made you deliver the check, too."

Jack looked incredulously at Riley, then at Hammond. "I don't know what you're talking about," he said. "I don't know anything about this guy, Hardin, or Sandi for that matter." He looked across the room.

"Jack! How could you," Sandi sounded hurt and burst into tears. "After all we've been through!" she blubbered.

"Yes, Mr. Casey," Riley said, "after all you've been through."

"We're going to get to the bottom of this," Hammond said, standing.

Riley also rose to his feet. "Yes, we will. So, don't you lovebirds go anywhere, okay? We'll be in touch."

As soon as the door shut behind the investigators Sandi was on her feet. She stormed down the hallway to what would have been her room and picked up her bag. Jack just stared. She strode to the door and, with her hand on the doorknob, turned to look back at Jack.

"How dare you!" she spat. "You are just as much a suspect as I am!"

With that, she was out the door, and Jack heard the Porsche roar down the street.

"Son of a...!" and a little voice inside whispered, *Language, Jack. Try to be good.*

"Like hell," he muttered to himself, regretting it immediately. *Sorry, Mom. And how am I supposed to get my car back?* 26

Chapter 26

Jack hopped in the cab and said, "Fairfax. You know where the international market is on Lee Highway?"

"You show me, okay?" the driver replied.

"Sure. Just take 28 back to 50, and I'll tell you where from there."

Thirty minutes later, Jack paid the cabbie and unlocked the door of his car. He noticed the assistant manager looking at him from the sidewalk in front of the store. Jack waved, and the man just stared.

What's with this town? Some kind of a curse?

He left the parking lot, turned right on Lee Highway and then right on Sandi's street. Although he had no desire to ever see her again, he did want a diet coke. He pulled into the 7-11. Walking straight to the back cooler, he grabbed what he wanted and made his way back to the counter.

"Is that it?" the familiar face asked. Jack stopped there often after work to quench his thirst before heading home.

"Yeah, just a coke."

"You don't want a lottery ticket? I just found out we sold a winner," the clerk said. "You could be next."

"You're kidding! Who won?"

"I don't know. I've been trying to think of who's been buying 'em. You know what, though? There's some guys used to come in every morning for coffee and junk, bought tickets every Friday, checked numbers every Monday. I haven't seen them since Monday. I think they won." He handed Jack change from the two dollars Jack had offered in payment.

"Lucky them," Jack said as he pocketed his change.

"Yeah, I bet they won. I mean, they were here every morning and bought tickets every Friday. Three guys, three tickets. Construction workers, carpenters or something. This has been going on for a couple years, maybe more. And now they don't show up Tuesday or Wednesday? I mean not just one is missing or two. None of them show up for two days. It's not like there's any shortage of work around. I'm waiting to see who claims the money."

"I wish it was me," Jack said. He pocketed his change and left.

Echols returned to the jail and asked to see Race.

"Alright, Mr. Echols. You know the drill. ID and wait. I'll have someone get him."

When they were together in the brightly lit but lusterless room where Race had been interrogated, Echols said, "I need your permission to get your belongings. His honor said when he has…when he has the money," Echols caught himself before he said $900,000. "Uh, then he'll set your bail. And I can get you out of here," he added, hoping to make the plan sound good to Race.

"You sorry ass," Race said, looking right into Echols eyes. "How do I know he'll set the bail? How do I know you'll even ask him to?"

"I will, I will," Echols pleaded. "What else can we do?"

Race thought, and after a moment said, "You write up a document that says you are collecting $11 million on my behalf. You get that check from the lottery made out to me. Show it to his honor," the phrase slipped out filled with derision. "When I'm out, he gets paid. You got that? And if you screw this up I'll kill you." His voice remained calm and cold.

"I'll type up the document myself. I'll go do that right now. Then I'll talk to the judge," Echols said rapidly. "I'll try to get all that done today, maybe even get the check today." His excitement overflowed.

"Just do it," Race said and stood. "I'm done " he shouted to the guard, but still looking at Echols.

"Are these murders even related?" Riley looked at his partner as he drove. "I can't find a motive for the two guys in the woods. The motel clerk was to cover his tracks. The mother, I don't think he did it, although he is a nut case."

Hammond just drove for a minute and finally said, "I don't know. I don't know why he killed those guys, but Casey and Anderson look good for the mother."

"But he killed those guys before he found his mother."

"We don't know that," Hammond replied. "Maybe he knew about his mother before. Maybe he just went out there to confirm."

"Maybe. We need more info. Let's check out Anderson's job situation. I'd be interested in hearing what her boss and co-workers think of her."

Hammond made a U-turn and headed back toward Dulles International Airport.

Julia walked into her apartment and offered a sullen greeting to Angel, who stood in front of the kitchen sink rinsing a soapy cloth.

"What's wrong, Julia? ¿Por que tan triste? Why so sad?"

"Oh, nothing. I'm just disappointed."

"Is the post office getting you down?"

Angel put down the cloth and dried his hands. He turned toward Julia and she gently collapsed in his arms, resting her head on his strong chest.

"You'll be okay," he soothed, "You'll be okay."

"Angel, why are men so shallow? Crei tener un amigo. I thought I had a friend."

"¡Hey, my little brokenhearted sister, Yo no soy un hombre mal! Now, who is this bad man who hurt you? You want me to beat him up?"

Angel's jokes were comforting and so were his arms, but Julia still hurt. She sighed and closed her eyes.

"You remember Jack? From the market? You saw me with him at the post office, too."

Angel tenderly pushed Julia to his arms' length and turned her face toward his.

"Stay away from him, Julia, please," he begged more than ordered. "He's in a lot of trouble. If what they say is true...well, just stay away from him. I know. I know you like him; he's your friend, but, Julia…just stay away from him."

"I will, Angel. But, hey, don't think it's because you told me to! I don't want you thinking you can give me orders!" Julia smiled and looked askance at her brother.

"That's better," Angel returned her smile. "Now, Miss 'I'm-in-control-of-my-own-life,' let's think about dinner."

"Okay, you cook."

"No, I just cleaned up from this morning."

"I cooked last night."

"But I cleaned."

They went to La Granja de Oro, their favorite Peruvian restaurant.

Jack walked out of the 7-11 and hopped in his car. He unscrewed the top from his bottle of coke and took a long pull at the sweet caffeine riddled nectar.

"Ahhh " and he belched.

He returned the lid to the bottle, hit the ignition and was rewarded with a 'click.'

"Crap!" and then he thought, *Oops! Ma, this good language thing isn't easy when you're having a crappy day.*

He walked back into the 7-11 and waited to the side of the register while the clerk waited on a couple of customers. They purchased drinks and asked for a lottery ticket.

When they left, he looked at Jack. "There goes another winner! I can just feel it."

"Well, that wouldn't be me, then," Jack said. "Can I bother you to jump start my car? It just died in front of your store," he motioned with his head and eyes. "I've got cables."

"Bummer! But, I can't," and the clerk looked up toward the security camera. "I'm the only one here right now. I can't leave, even to go out front."

"Oh. Shoot. I guess I'll call for a jump. Thanks anyway."

The clerk looked at Jack for a moment and then said, "Hold on. I think I can trust you. Besides, I know where you work." He reached in his pocket and tossed his car keys on the counter. "It's the dirty Nissan by the Dumpster. Probably belongs in the Dumpster, but at least it starts." He and Jack laughed.

"Thanks, man. You just saved me about fifty bucks. I owe you."

"Don't worry about it."

Jack got his car started and re-parked the Nissan. On his way back in, to return the keys, he noticed a front-page story on a local newspaper just inside the door:

DOUBLE HOMICIDE NEAR RESERVOIR

The story recounted George and Eddie's demise, and, by way of background information, said they were carpenters on a local construction project.

"Construction workers," Jack said to himself. He grabbed a paper and spoke to the clerk as he walked over to the counter. "Thanks again," he said, and quickly added, "lemme get this paper."

"Sure, sure anytime. The paper's fifty-cents."

Jack already had section A open on the counter and found the continued story inside. There was a picture of George, looking very much the family man, and one of Eddie, looking posed, hung-over and uncomfortable.

"Are these the guys who bought the lottery tickets every Friday?" Jack turned the paper around for his friend behind the counter.

The man looked at Jack, then at the paper, and looked surprised. "I'll be damned! That's two of them." He looked at Jack, puzzled. "How did you know?"

"Just, uh, one of them lived on my route. I kind of knew he was missing and this article caught my eye."

"No wonder they haven't been in! They're dead! Where's the third guy?" the clerk asked, and the question hung between them.

Chapter 27

Hammond and Riley sat in a small, utilitarian office across the desk from one of the ticket agent supervisors for United Airlines at Dulles International Airport.

"Yes, she has been a good employee. Average really. She doesn't miss work often; however she is off this week. She called and said there was some sort of family emergency," the middle aged, uniformed woman looked up at the detectives as if she had asked a question.

"Does she get along with her co-workers?" Riley asked.

"Yes. Yes she does. Never any problem in that respect."

"Does she have close friends?"

"No, not really. She keeps to herself. There's really not much I can tell you."

"Any financial problems that you're aware of?"

"No, not really. She pretty much kept to herself."

"Dead end," Hammond said as they headed back to Fairfax.

"Yeah, like the rest of this case."

Echols had the formal IOU in his hand as he approached the glass enclosure to the jail.

"I need to see Race Hardin again," he said to the guard on the other side of the glass.

"Who? I don't think we have any 'Race,' or did you mean 'Ace?' I need a formal name." There had been a shift change.

"Of course, 'John R. Hardin' is who I need to see. Sorry," Echols said.

Within minutes, Echols and Race were face to face: Race on one side of the table in shackles and Echols on the other.

"I got the agreement. I just need your signature," Echols spoke rapidly. He was nervous. He had been nervous since he found out about the ticket.

"Calm down, Echols," Race said as he took the paper from the attorney.

After a few moments of reading, Race said, "Alright. I'll sign it, but you remember who you're dealing with." he gave Echols a look that sent a chill right through the disheveled public counselor.

"See if you can get me out of here tonight."

"But, there's not enough time."

"Then do it first thing in the morning," Race said. The words came out like a strand of steel. He stood and a guard took him away.

Echols nearly ran through the halls of justice on his way to show the judge the ticket. He had taken a written statement signed by Race to the guard on duty. The document gave Echols permission to retrieve Races personal effects from the property room. Now, halfway to the judge's chambers, he realized that the judge wanted to see money, not tickets. Besides, his honor had probably gone home for the day.

Tomorrow, first thing, I'll go to the lottery commission and get a check; then to the bank; then to the judge.

Jack drove home wondering: *Did those guys win the lottery? Is that why two of them are dead? Did Sandi know anything about it? And, if they won, where is the lottery ticket? And who killed Hardin's mother? How can I prove I didn't?*

Chapter 28

Riley walked into the diner on Lee Highway and slid into the booth across from Hammond. John Hammond had finished eating and nursed a strong cup of coffee, his second.

"Sorry, partner," Riley spoke, smelling of soap and damp hair. "Gotta get my beauty rest, ya know?"

"It's not working," Hammond replied. It was a rare attempt at humor from the detective.

"What? The apology or the beauty rest?"

Hammond almost smiled while Riley perused the menu.

"You think it's changed since last time?" Hammond asked.

Riley stopped and stared quixotically at his long time sidekick.

"You're in rare form this morning," he said to the big man. "Have you been bothering Mrs. Hammond?"

Now Hammond smiled and almost laughed.

"No, I've been talking to the guys at the jailhouse about our homicidal friend, Mr. Hardin. His attorney was in and out a few times yesterday. They were exchanging documents apparently and swapping Hardin's personal belongings for a sealed envelope. They're up to something. Let's give Echols enough time to make a motion and then go see the judge. I think something's going to break."

"You sure do talk a lot," Riley smiled, "but first let's eat."

"You go ahead," Hammond said over his egg stained plate.

After Riley had eaten he said, "So you think something's up, huh?"

"Lot's of last minute dealings; they're going to try something today."

"And if it's a plan to spring him, then what?"

"We follow him," Hammond said, and one corner of his mouth turned up.

"I don't want to lose this guy, John. We got him dead to rights for three murders, just no motive. You know, with the evidence we have, we don't need motive."

"We won't lose him. I want motive. On top of everything else, I want motive."

"We may never find out, you know, John?" Riley said. "Let's check with the judge and keep an eye on those two, but let's rattle the little love-bird cage, too. Those two had motive and means. We just need to prove they did it."

"Why are you so serious today?" Hammond asked. "You called me 'John' twice."

♠

Echols woke up early and got out of bed, despite his hangover. Over the last twenty years, the hangover had become habitual. He had spent last night at home alone, except for the bottle of scotch, now lying empty on the table by his La-Z-Boy recliner.

Frequent rasping groans accompanied him toward the bathroom along with an exclamatory bray as he slipped and nearly fell on a pornographic magazine. He remained oblivious to his own pain-filled utterances as he stumbled toward the shower. Living alone was conducive to talking, or groaning, out loud without being aware of it.

"Gotta get going," he muttered. "Gotta get to the State Lottery Commission as soon as they open."

Echols needed to go to Woodbridge if he wanted to cash in with the State Lottery office; they opened at 8:30 AM. Otherwise, he could go to any branch of Bank of America, but he wanted to go straight to the source; the bank would probably just leave him standing around while they contacted the lottery anyway.

By 7:30 AM, Echols joined the hordes of commuters on the byways of Fairfax and surrounding counties. But he headed toward a bigger payday than the rest: the Prize Zone at the Lottery Office on Potomac Mills Road in Woodbridge.

Julia labored in the PO Box section of the post office, sorting the mail into the appropriate boxes as quickly as she could. She heard a box key scrape and a door open, and the mail in a box for Ray's Painting disappeared. Julia continued working and after a moment a voice from the lobby shouted through the open box.

"Hey! Is this all the mail for today?"

"No, sir," Julia called back. "I still have some to sort. Can you come back in one hour? I will be finished by then." She hadn't spoken out loud at all this morning, and her thoughts had all been in Spanish. Now she exuded a Latin accent.

"No, I can't come back in an hour, goddamit! Maybe if you could read English you'd be finished by now."

She heard the little door snap shut, and someone shuffled away complaining about 'no f—ing check.'

¿Donde esta mi amigo? Where is my friend when I need a friend? she thought, and then remembered what Angel had said about Jack.

She also remembered what she had seen at Jack's house, but part of her still held hope: hope that Jack was not a criminal; hope that Jack didn't have anything to do with 'that gringa;' hope that they still had a chance.

I shouldn't be this way, she thought. *Jack has his own life, and whoever that girl is,...well, I shouldn't be this way.*

Julia continued working, and occasionally during the day she would smile and speak to her co-workers. But she missed that special feeling that comes from being with special people. She missed Jack.

Judge Deaber followed his normal working-day routine, but a twinge of excitement mingled with the commonplace. His slumber had been shallow, interrupted by indigestion and a couple of trips to the bathroom. Now he felt tired and a little queasy. The fatigue was normal; feeling ill was not.

I wonder if that jackass, Echols, will follow through with the money he promised. I doubt it, and I feel like hell. Maybe I should just stay home today, he thought.

But he didn't stay home; he went to work, as usual. Except he had a little hope. Just a little.

Jack didn't need an alarm clock. His head told him it was time for some Tylenol.

What a crappy way to spend a week off, he thought.

He stumbled to the bathroom, much like Echols had, only without tripping on any pornography. He fumbled to get the childproof lid off the painkiller and swallowed three with a palm full of water from the tap. Actually, Jack's head injury caused less suffering than the drunken attorney's hangover, but when it's your head that hurts, it feels worse than anyone else's. Besides, Jack wasn't accustomed to waking up feeling awful. Not since he quit drinking.

He relieved himself, started the shower and stepped under the warm baptismal spray, welcoming him back to life.

That's better, he thought. He dressed and felt almost human as he walked to the kitchen. *Now for some coffee,* Jack continued his normal morning approach to a day off, but nagging thoughts of being a murder suspect ruined his peace of mind. *I need to find out what's going on with that murder investigation. I might need to clear myself. Those two detectives would just as soon pin it on me as anyone else. And I'm curious. Did Race kill those other two guys for a lottery ticket? And if he did, where is it?*

The phone rang.

"Hello?"

"Jack? This is Sandi. Don't hang up."

"Okay," Jack said, wondering. "What can I do for you? Did you forget something?"

"No, Jack. Look, those two detectives think we had something to do with Race's mother's death. We have to prove that he did it. I know you don't care for me, Jack, but please, help. We're in this together."

"Sandi, I haven't done anything wrong. So far, all my problems stem from being around you and Hardin."

"Please, Jack. They still think we are tied up in this together. You've got to help clear us."

"No, Sandi, I don't. I only need to clear me."

A pause weighted the conversation. When Sandi spoke again her voice became poisoned with animosity.

"If you don't help me, Jack, I'll tell the detectives that you killed Race's mother and made me cash the social security checks."

The threat nearly flattened Jack. It was worse than the beating he had taken at the hands of this woman's ex-lover. Silence hung heavy on the phone line.

"I expect to hear from you before I hear from the police, Jack, or I will tell them you did it."

A click and, after a moment, a dial tone concluded the call.

Chapter 29

Echols headed toward Woodbridge from Fairfax. Traffic everywhere crawled, as usual, but Echols hadn't commuted in years. Frustration and anxiety ate at his psyche, and he fumed. He had just spilled coffee on himself, hitting the brakes hard after accelerating too quickly. He thought the jam had broken, but it hadn't.

"Damn it!" he said, feeling invisible in his car. "I'm still stuck in traffic, and now this. Just what I needed: wet pants."

Traffic inched along, and Echols decided to get off of Little River Turnpike. He would try Braddock Road. He had almost reached a right turn lane near the Northern Virginia Community College when the creeping traffic halted again.

"Son of a bitch!" Echols exclaimed, and jerked his wheel to the right.

The front of his car bumped onto the shoulder just as a student, late for class, roared up the gravel roadside and plowed into him. The impact pushed him into the back of the car he had been following. The student's car careened into the ditch.

Judge Deaber sat quietly in his chamber thinking:

I'll believe it when I see it. Echols is a moron. Still, if he shows up with anything, I'll be ready.

He prepared a release form for John Racine Hardin on $1,000,000 bail and slipped it into his brief case.

Nothing that says I need to sign this right now. I don't think I could anyway.

The judge felt achy with pain shooting up his arm.

Maybe I should lie down, he thought.

Hammond and Riley headed toward Sterling, VA to see if they could rattle Jack enough to make him slip. Maybe he would spill some information, something incriminating.

While Hammond and Riley traveled to his house, Jack drove his old Chevy to Fairfax. Jack and the detectives passed each other, unaware.

I've got to get that woman off my back. I don't know if she killed that guy's mother or not, but I know I didn't.

Echols climbed into the tow truck beside the driver, a big, round, dirty man with unkempt hair and beard. Echols didn't want to talk to the man, so he pretended to read his just-issued ticket. He had been charged with driving on the shoulder of the road. The student who ran into him had an identical citation. The innocent driver, the one Echols had been pushed into, would have his car repaired at Echols' and the student's expense. But being blameless and receiving free repairs offered little to make up for the ruined car or the ruined day. The man's patience in traffic had been replaced with anger toward Echols and the kid.

"This is the second time in twelve months that I've been rear-ended because I stopped for traffic. This is the kind of stupidity that jacks up insurance rates for everyone in Northern Virginia," he complained bitterly to the officer on the scene.

Statistically, the constant traffic jams in the area propelled it into the top ten on the list of 'worst in the nation' for commuters.

Now Echols sat staring at the piece of paper the officer had handed him, and he smelled the grease that coated the cab of the truck and the driver. His suit would be ruined for sure.

What the hell does it matter, he thought. *I just need to get to Woodbridge and back, see the judge, and get my client out of jail. I can buy a new suit with $100,000.*

"I can take you up University Drive after lunch if you want to wait at the shop," the driver said.

He spoke as he towed Echols' car back toward Fairfax; his looks belied his articulate speech.

"I have to pick up a car at Jim Mckay Chevrolet anyway."

"No," Echols growled. And then, realizing that the man was only offering a kindness, he added, "I can walk from here, probably quicker than I could get a cab. But thanks. I appreciate the offer."

Jack pulled into the Shell station just outside of Fairfax's historical district. After inserting his charge card into the gas pump, he quickly removed it and started pumping gas. He stood by the back of his car; the heat made sitting in it nearly impossible.

He watched the tow truck pull in and two men got out. One wore a suit, but he didn't look any better than the disheveled driver.

Actually, with that frown on his face, he looks worse, Jack thought. *I guess the banged up car has something to do with that.*

Jack watched the two go separate ways, but the driver turned back and shouted, "You sure you don't want to wait for a ride? It's awfully hot."

Echols waved him off. "No, I'm kind of in a hurry, and it's just up University Drive a little ways. Thanks any way."

Jack watched the man fumble with his brief case and trousers, trying to tuck his shirttail in with one hand.

He is having a bad day. I guess I could help him out. I'm heading that direction anyway. An afterthought occurred, *and I can actually do something decent, other than refraining from profanity. For you, Mom, okay?*

Jack walked over to the red-faced man. "I heard where you're heading. I'm going over to Lee Highway anyway. Want a ride? It's no problem."

Echols started to say 'no', but hesitated. "I...well..."

"Come on. You look like you're having a crappy day. Believe me, I've been there. Hop in."

Echols shuffled to Jack's car and climbed in on the passenger's side. "Thanks. I am kind of in a hurry. This will help, a lot. Actually, if I could ride with you to Lee Highway, I think there's a car rental place up by Kamp Washingtion."

"Yeah," Jack said and fired the engine. "I know exactly where it is. I can drop you there."

It was a short ride without much conversation, both men lost in their own thoughts, searching for ways to change their futures. Jack pulled into the Hertz car lot and up to the small office.

"Here you go," he said and put the car in park.

"Thanks," Echols muttered and reached awkwardly for his wallet and his briefcase and the door handle, all at once.

"Not necessary," Jack said, seeing the attempt to extract money from the billfold. "This is on my way."

"You sure? I'd like to give you something, at least for gas," Echols said looking up at Jack and still fingering the money."

"I'm sure," Jack said and added, "Just have a better rest of the day."

"I gotta give you something," Echols said, and pushed a few bills into Jacks shirt pocket.

Jack laughed. "If you insist, but really, I'm okay."

"Buy yourself a beer."

With that, Echols was out of the car and moving toward the rental office.

"Our boy's not home," Riley said.

Hammond just looked at him.

"No sense hanging around here. Let's check Lover-girl's house; see if either of them is there; or both of them."

"Hurry up, before the steering wheel cooks again," Hammond said, already two steps toward the cruiser.

Chapter 30

Jack made a right turn, went up the road a quarter of a mile and turned right again. He drove through Sandi's neighborhood and saw her expensive car in the gravel pull-in.

Not yet, he thought. *I don't want to talk to her yet.*

He drove by slowly and headed back toward Lee Highway. He pulled in at the 7-11, the one where his car wouldn't start; the same one where Race, George and Eddie bought their lottery tickets. He parked in front of the door and hurried from the car to the air-conditioned store. A bell clanged as he pushed the door open and let it go.

"Hey, man," the clerk said, looking up from a newspaper.

"Hey," Jack answered and headed for the cooler in back.

He grabbed a 20-ounce Diet-Coke and brought it up to counter.

"Where's that other guy that works here?" Jack asked. "He did me a big favor the other day when my car wouldn't start."

"Oh, yeah?" the clerk rang up the coke without looking at Jack. "He's off today. That's a dollar and thirty-nine cents," he said and looked up.

Jack reached in the front pocket of his jeans and came up empty.

"Aw, shiii…" and he caught himself. *I almost said it,* he thought. *Sorry, Mom.* Then to the clerk, "left my wallet in the car. "Oh, hold on a sec," he said and reached into his shirt pocket where Echols had stuffed the bills. "Here we go," and he put the wad on the counter and began straightening out the paper.

There were three one-dollar bills, and, in between them, there was a lottery ticket.

"Oh, check it out. A lottery ticket. Wonder if it's worth anything."

"I can let you know real quick," the clerk said and picked up the ticket.

He ran it through the electronic device behind the counter, stared for a moment, and said, "I don't believe it! You better sit down for this!"

"Sit down for what?" Jack asked.

"Well, let's just say you don't have to worry about your car not starting anymore," and he handed Jack the ticket with a printout.

Jack looked closely at what he held in his hand and nearly fell over. He looked at the clerk and opened his mouth, but nothing came out.

"What are you gonna do?" the clerk said through a smile so big it could have swallowed his face.

"Oh, my God! Is this for real?"

"Yeah, man, it's for real!"

"Oh, my God!"

Jack looked back at the ticket, then back at the clerk, and then stumbled out of the store. He was opening his car door when the clerk caught him.

"Here's your coke, man. I called you but I guess you were preoccupied." The clerk's smile verged on laughter now.

"Yeah. Thanks. Wow."

The clerk walked back in and Jack climbed into his car. He started it and drove back to Sandi's neighborhood, but not to her house. He went to the next block over and stopped in front of a little park; the same little park Race had parked George's truck in front of only a few days earlier.

Okay, Mom, Jack began. *What are we going to do with this guy's ticket? Does he know it's a winner? But I thought Hardin had the ticket. Who was that guy I dropped off?* And, of course, the inevitable underlying thought surfaced: *I could just keep this, Mom. He gave it to me and said to buy myself a beer. It's mine.*

Hammond and Riley pulled to the curb in front of Sandi's bungalow.

"I don't see Casey's car, but that doesn't mean anything. The Porsche was the only car at his house yesterday. Let's see who's home," Riley said and exited the big Ford.

He and Hammond crossed the yard and climbed the steps to the front door. Televised laughter greeted them from somewhere beyond the door.

They looked at each other, and Riley knocked. They waited and he knocked again. The volume of the television decreased rapidly. Finally Sandi opened the door. She looked rumpled, her cheek embossed with a pillow design.

"I...I was sleeping. Why are you here?"

"Sorry we woke you," Riley said. "I don't suppose Jack Casey is here, is he?"

"N-no. He...I...we...left. I left. Him. He's at home, isn't he?"

"No. We were just there," Riley said. "Could we come in for a minute, Sandi. May I call you Sandi?"

"Okay," she said and pulled the door all the way open.

Hammond and Riley exchanged glances and stepped inside.

Judge Deaber sat at his desk looking at a brown paper bag that contained his lunch.

I knew that bastard, Echols, wouldn't come through. I'm going to be stuck brown bagging for the rest of my life.

He pushed the bag aside and pulled out the bail-release for John Hardin and looked at it. He almost ran it through the shredder, but thought twice.

The day isn't over, he thought. *I'll give him until this afternoon.*

He placed the form on his desk and thought about lying down on the sofa. He didn't feel well. He began to push up from the desk but couldn't. A sharp pain gripped his chest, and he clutched at his heart. The few seconds of suffering seemed endless, but eventually his head came to rest on Race Hardin's bail release.

Race picked up a tray in the cafeteria of the Fairfax County jail. He was livid.

"Watch it, shithead" the guy in line in front of him turned back to face him.

Race had accidentally bumped him with the tray. The man looked like a killer, tattooed and snarling. He stood two inches taller than Race and outweighed him by forty pounds. He seemed to be the big fish in this pond, but Race's tolerance for fools had reached an all-time low. The guy's forty extra pounds looked like it was all fat and the bluster appeared to come from too much beer.

The cafeteria became a little less noisy and most eyes turned toward the two men. Race stared straight into the other man's eyes.

"It was an accident."

"I don't care if it was your boyfriend behind you, you…"

Race swung the tray backhanded and it flew like a Frisbee across the room. The big man stepped back to avoid being hit and watched it sail. Taking his eyes off Race was a mistake. His nose broke and before he could focus, Race took him to the ground. He hit the tile hard, flat on his back.

The wind had been knocked out of him. He had three loose teeth and a broken jaw before the guards pulled Race off. Race's only injury appeared to be cut knuckles on his right hand.

"Get him to solitary and him to the infirmary. The rest of you ladies, sit down and eat."

Race smiled, but he was thinking, *Fucking Echols. You better get me out of here.*

Chapter 31

William Echols hopped in a rental car and looked for the place to put the key.

"Damn!" he nearly shouted.

I need to take it easy. Calm down, calm down, he told himself.

He took a moment to familiarize himself with the car and then started it.

I'll go see Judge Deaber first and tell him why I'm running late. I'll make sure he knows this is really going to happen.

He pulled off the car rental lot onto Lee Highway and headed to Chain Bridge Road. It would take him to the courthouse.

Jack's conscience tore at him, the way two cats will tear at each other. He felt like someone had run his guts through a shredder.

There's no choice, he thought. *I've got to find out who that guy is.* And the whole time he was thinking, another voice coerced him: *Don't! You can keep it. He doesn't know, or even if he does, too bad. Or give him half, and he's lucky to get that. It's his own fault. Get the money first.*

Jack drove through the maelstrom of thoughts toward the Shell station where he had picked the stranger up. A voice on the radio vied for his attention:

"...but the winner has yet to come forward."

Jack switched the radio off and turned into the gas station. He pulled over to the side and parked.

They might not want to give me his name, Jack thought.

He sat wondering what to do and suddenly realized the car next to him was the strangers damaged vehicle. The tow truck driver had backed it in and left it. Jack could see it wasn't locked; besides, the windows were down. He got out of his car and glanced toward the office and the garage. A young woman sat behind the counter at the register smoking and reading a magazine. Two mechanics spoke on one side of the garage, while a third stood under a lift, elbow deep in someone's problem. Jack walked around the damaged vehicle and got in on the passenger's side. In the glove box he found the car registration under a mess of paper and pens, a tire gauge and some matches.

William Echols, 2837 University Drive. That's easy. I'll drive by, maybe leave him a note.

"Can I help you with somethin'?"

Jack's head jerked up and his knee hit the glove box door. He was looking at one of the mechanics, and the other two in the garage were looking at him.

"Uh, no. I, uh...." Jack had no idea what to say.

"Oh, you're that guy who gave Mr. Echols a ride. He forget somethin'?"

"Yeah," Jack laughed softly. "You could say that. But I got it. Hope you don't mind," Jack said as he flipped the glove box closed.

"No, that's okay, so long as you don't take the car before the bill gets paid," the mechanic said and stepped back so Jack could get out.

"Thanks," Jack offered and he and the mechanic walked away from the car in different directions.

"It's that guy who gave Echols a ride," Jack heard the mechanic yell as he headed back to the garage. "Just forgot somethin' in the car.

Jack swung into his own car and saw the men in the garage return to what they had been doing. He started the engine and headed two blocks west to University drive. Main Street split and became one way streets in either direction, just long enough to get traffic through the historic part of town. Jack turned right on University and was out of the commercial district within a block. He knew about where Echols address would be, he just didn't know what he would do when he got there.

He's probably not there, anyway, Jack thought. *After all, I dropped him off at the car rental.*

But indecision nagged at Jack as he looked for street numbers on houses and mailboxes.

I guess some people just don't want to be found, Jack thought, as he passed houses with no numbers, or undecipherable numbers, or numbers in such out of the way places they were unlikely to ever be seen.

But suddenly, on his left, Jack saw it. A small sign stood in the front yard with clearly legible letters and numbers:

William Echols
Attorney at Law
2837 University Drive

A telephone number appeared at the bottom of the sign, and Jack knew he had no excuse for not contacting the man. He pulled into the empty driveway and sat. After one huge sigh, Jack got out and went to the door. He knocked, waited, and knocked again. No one came to the door, and the house emitted no sound. There was not a hint of anyone inside.

The nagging voice Jack had heard earlier came back:
You tried. Now just keep the ticket.
Another voice said, *You're a suspect in a murder case. Do something about it.*

And Jack heard himself say, "Shut up!" out loud as he returned to his car. He backed up enough to read the sign in the yard and found a pen and some paper. He recorded the attorney's name, address and phone number.

Now, I better go see those two detectives. I'd like to tell them what Sandi is trying to do.

He backed out of the driveway and headed back toward town.

Chapter 32

Without any encouragement, Sandi offered, "There's something I've got to tell you."

"I'm all ears," Riley replied, and added, "We need all the help we can get."

"I've been involved in...in..." and the tears came, and the wailing and sobbing. "I was afraid. I didn't know what he would do."

Hammond's eyes grew and he glanced at Riley, but Riley's focus centered on the woman sitting across from him. She leaned forward and her hands covered her face. She needed a tissue. Riley rose and offered her his handkerchief. He put his hand on her shoulder to comfort her.

"Let us help you. Take your time and tell us what happened. If you were coerced or threatened, then it's not your fault. Just tell us what happened."

"Thank you," Sandi blubbered, and blew her nose on Riley's handkerchief.

"Whenever you're ready, Ms. Anderson," Riley said.

He still hadn't looked at Hammond. John Hammond took in the scene with skepticism. He had seen enough tears in his career to know that not all of them were sincere. He wasn't sure about Sandi's, but he knew his partner had been taken in. Riley believed every word she was whimpering. It was either that, or he was doing a better job of acting than usual.

"I don't know where to start," Sandi finally managed, regaining some composure. "Those checks just caught his eye. I didn't think anything of it."

"Okay, caught whose eye? You mean the Social Security checks?"

"Yes. Jack always delivered them, and sometimes on weekends I would see him. He asked about them, you know? Like whose they were? I told him they belonged to Race's mother, and then I told him I took care of her. I never should have told him that, but I was complaining. Race wouldn't have anything to do with her. I don't know how they did it before I met him, but after we got together, I offered to check on her and pay her bills and buy her groceries, you know, everything."

She blew her nose again, and Riley offered the platitude, 'take your time,' as he wrote in his notebook. Hammond continued to study them both.

"One Saturday when Jack delivered our mail, I complained about things at Thelma's house, just upkeep, like squeaky doors and stuff like that. He was so nice and offered to help. I offered to pay him, like anyone, you know, a plumber or anybody who fixes things. I told him it would come out of her check. After that, he went with me to her house a few times. He cut the grass and fixed a few things around the house, and I paid him.

Anyway, he knew where she lived and helped out with other stuff that needed to be done, but I guess he was just checking it out."

Now Hammond and Riley both focused completely on Sandi's story.

Sandi continued, "He started going up there by himself on his days off, and he would just tell me how much to pay him. Finally, one day, he said, 'Don't go out there anymore. Thelma is dead.' I was shocked. She was old, but she was fine the last time I saw her. I was still buying groceries and cleaning the house, so I went out there at least once a week."

"Then Jack told me not to say anything to anybody. He said I should keep on cashing the checks, and we would split the money. I said I couldn't, but he insisted. He grabbed my arm and..." the tears began again. "H-h-he threatened me," and Sandi broke down completely. Through her sobs she blurted, "He said if I told anyone I would end up like Thelma," and her crying continued.

Riley rose and put his arm around her shoulders pulling her close to contain her quaking.

"It's okay, it's not your fault," he cooed, and finally he looked at Hammond.

Hammond could see that Riley believed every word of the story. He leaned toward believing it, too, but he would like to hear Jack Casey's side. He decided to keep his thoughts to himself for the time being.

Jack took University Drive back toward the historical old town of Fairfax. The courthouse and the jail stood there, besieged by office buildings ranging in age from modern to 150 years old. Main Street held its boutiques, bars and bail bondsmen; the office buildings were filled mostly with attorneys dealing with the legal trials and tribulations of a large and densely populated county.

One block before Main Street, Jack turned right on a one way street that skirted old town. He could drive by the Post Office without going much out of his way and follow Page Avenue right back to the jail. Someone there or in the connected courthouse would know where he could find detectives Hammond and Riley. And maybe Julia would be at the Post Office. If she got off on time, she would be leaving soon.

I don't want to go in there, Jack thought. *I'm probably not supposed to, anyway. I'm suspended,* and his thoughts turned briefly to Morey and his suspension.

He passed the front of the Post Office and drove around to the side where he could see the employees' parking lot. He pulled to the curb and stopped by the 'No Parking' sign. He used his side-view mirror to see who came and went through the back door of the building.

He could see Julia's car parked close to the door; she was always among the first few employees to arrive. He wanted to see her. He wanted to straighten out her misconception of the situation at his house. He wanted to tell her that he wasn't and had never been involved with Sandi; that he hadn't done anything wrong; that it was all a big mistake.

It was important to Jack that she knew, even if they never shared another thing. Julia's opinion of his character somehow rose above Jack's other priorities. She had become for Jack his most important friend. He would have given up all his other friends and acquaintances to keep her friendship.

Who am I kidding. I don't have any other friends.

Even so, she was different. He had known women who satisfied his lust, and he had known women who were pals, but he had never known a woman he could trust completely. Julia represented Jack's every ideal in a woman. He marveled at the depth of his feelings toward her.

Where did all this come from?

Movement in the mirror shattered his reverie. Two women left the building together, laughing as they walked. They parted ways, each going to their own car, and shouted 'see ya later' before climbing in.

Jack's adrenaline level quickly sank back to normal, only to spike again as the door opened. Julia walked out, head down, with one hand holding her purse and the other digging around in it.

This is it, Jack thought as he opened his car door and stepped out.

Julia found her keys, opened her car door and settled in. Jack stood in the street, 200 feet away and watched. He stood near the only exit to the parking lot.

Julia backed out and headed for the exit. She had slowed and looked right and left and would have gone right, but Jack's sharp voice caused her to stop abruptly. Jack crossed the street toward her. She waited, but the look on her face appeared uninviting.

"Julia, can I talk to you," Jack said in a voice just short of pleading. "I…"

"I'm not supposed to talk to you, Jack," Julia replied coldly. "They say you are in trouble."

"I didn't do whatever you heard, Julia. I just wanted you to know that."

"Well, okay, Jack, whatever you say. Maybe you should just go see your friend con el pelo rubio," Julia said with her eyes looking straight ahead, and now a hint of anger and betrayal tinged her voice.

"'Con el pelo rubio'?" Jack asked, a question directed more at himself than Julia.

Before he could translate, a voice came from behind him: "Is this your car?"

Jack turned and saw what Julia had already seen: a Fairfax City Police sedan sat between Jack and his illegally parked car.

"Uh, yeah. Can I have just a minute?" Jack asked.

"No! The sign says 'no parking,' and it means 'no parking'," the officer called irritably.

"Julia, meet me somewhere, please," Jack begged.

"I can't Jack," Julia replied without looking at him. "I have to go."

Julia pulled out of the parking lot and drove off.

"Move it or lose it," the ill-tempered voice said.

Jack turned away from watching Julia leave and looked at the scowling officer across the street.

"Yeah, yeah," he said, moving toward his car but looking down the road as Julia turned toward Main Street.

Chapter 33

William Echols parked the rental in the parking garage across the street from the courthouse and was nearly clipped by a car in his hurry to the building. He entered on the lower level and impatiently waited his turn at the metal detector. Finally, having successfully navigated the basket, conveyor belt and electronic pulse field, he charged upstairs to the main level. From there, he took the two-story escalator to the next level where the courtrooms and judges' chambers were located.

He's probably in court. I'll leave him a note. I gotta get this to work, Echols thought as he charged down the hallway to Judge Deaber's office.

He reached the office door and knocked, just to be sure, then tried the doorknob. The door opened. Echols slipped in and turned back to softly shut the door behind him. The whole time, he thought about how to say what he needed to say without leaving any incriminating evidence.

He rotated to face the desk, looking for a note pad and a good place to leave the note. Instead, he found himself staring at the top of Judge Deaber's head.

Oh, crap, Echols thought. *He's taking a nap. I'd better leave.* But he thought better of the idea. *No, I've got to let him know, to get Hardin out today.*

He tiptoed to the desk. It was a foolish thing to do since he intended to wake the Judge anyway.

"Your Honor," he almost whispered. Then he repeated himself, but much louder: "Your Honor." He reached out in a moment of audacity and touched the Judge's shoulder. "Judge Deaber," he pleaded. He shook the limp form in front of him. Nothing happened. "Judge Deaber, are you okay," but Echols was beginning to realize that the Judge was not okay.

He felt the Judge's neck for a pulse. His Honor was cold to the touch. His heart was not beating, and he wasn't breathing.

No, no, no! Echols thought, and then he noticed the 'Release on Bail' form beneath the Judge's head.

Gently, he lifted the cranium of the now deceased Judge and slipped the bail form out from under it. It looked complete except for the missing signature.

"I can fix that," he muttered, unaware that he had spoken.

He no longer paid any attention to the dead man. He focused totally on the paper in his hand, the means to an end.

"I can still get the money."

Race lay on his cot in solitary, a picture of yogic calm. But, in fact, he contained enough of the venom of anger and hatred to demolish a man's sanity.

You had better hurry Echols," he thought, *while you still have a chance. I will find a way to reach you.*

Julia drove and held back tears. It was sad to lose a friend.

Tu me pones triste, mi amigo. Quiero saber el porqué, Jack.

When she arrived at the apartment, Angel was preparing for work.

"Is that you, Julia?" Angel called.

"Yes, my dear brother," she answered, but she sounded tired and annoyed.

"What's the matter?"

Angel stopped buttoning his shirt and walked to where Julia had dropped her purse and lunch utensils on the kitchen counter. She wouldn't look at him, so he took her chin in his hand and gently turned her head toward him and tilted her face up towards his. Julia closed her eyes.

"Don't make me get rough," he whispered.

Julia laughed, but it was a sad laugh.

"I miss my friend, Jack, Angel. I don't think he's bad. What do they say he did? And who is that blonde gringa?"

"Oh, I see. You are jealous."

Julia smirked and looked away. "I just don't think he's a bad man, Angel. And, yes, I'm jealous. Why should the blonde, y blanca have all the fun. I'm getting old, you know."

"Oh, yes, claro. The wrinkles are forming as we speak. Julia, cariñosa, you are young and smart and pretty. Stop pushing away the good men who come to you. You don't need someone like Casey."

"But what did he do, Angel. Tell me."

"He's involved in some bad stuff, hermana. People have died. I don't know if he's totally responsible, but he's involved somehow. Just stay away from him, okay? Don't make me worry, or I'll have as many wrinkles as you."

Instinctively, he retreated into the living room and threw up his arms in defense. Julia pummeled him with a cushion from the sofa.

Angel left for work, and Julia wondered: *What is really going on, Jack? Are you in trouble?*

Julia turned on the radio in the kitchen after Angel left for work. She got a glass from the cabinet and opened the freezer to access the pile of funny shaped ice-pieces from the automatic icemaker. She added cola and started cleaning the kitchen, though there was little to do. Eventually she sat in the living room, set her drink on the end table by the sofa, and stared out the balcony door at the passing traffic on Route 50.

¡Ay! El tràfico.

Julia reached for her drink and knocked something onto the floor between the table and couch. Curious, she leaned forward and peered under the table.

Angel! How can I reach you if you don't carry your cell phone? Well, today I can reach you anyway, my brother. You told me you would be in traffic court in Fairfax.

She reached under the table and folded her fingers around Angel's phone.

I'll just take it to him. He can't get away from me that easily.

She smiled. It would be nice to see him while he worked. And it would be nice to see him working in the courthouse for a change—a safe environment.

Jack drove up Page Avenue and, without realizing it, parked next to Echols' car in the parking garage by the jail and courthouse. It smelled of moist concrete and motor oil with a hint of the fumes of spent fuel. People in a variety of cars came and went, raising and lowering the gates and paying at the automated ticket machines.

I guess he would be in one of the court rooms, Jack thought with Echols in mind. *I wonder if he's missed the winning ticket yet. I wonder if he even knows it's a winning ticket.*

Jack proceeded out of the parking garage and across the street to the courthouse. He negotiated the same metal detector that Echols had encountered, and he walked a flight of stairs and then rode the escalator to the courtrooms.

I suppose I can ask around, or just peak in on a trial or two.

Chapter 34

"Come with me, Hardin," the officer said in a flat voice.

Race rose from the cot in his cell. His eyes never left the deputy.

He doesn't look big or dangerous, the deputy told himself, but he would do as he was told. *Better safe than fired,* he thought, so he said, "Three of us are going to escort you, in shackles, to the courthouse. Judge Deaber wants to see you."

This better be my ticket out of here, Race thought, but he said nothing.

One of two officers in the hallway entered the cell carrying chains and locks. The second officer followed with his nightstick drawn. After letting the other two in, the first officer removed his nightstick from his belt.

"I'm told you are a bad man," he offered in a flat tone. He knew better than to bait his charge. "We can do this the easy way if you like," he said, tilting his head toward the shackles.

Race's eyes pierced the distance between them with a steel hard gaze that seemed as if it would puncture the man's face. "Alright," Race said, amiably, and held out his hands as he spread his feet. His eyes never left his captor.

The three officers exchanged glances and then the two wielding night sticks looked at the man holding the chains. He gave them an 'oh well' kind of look and proceeded to cuff Race's hands. Race relaxed and allowed the man to chain him, hand and foot.

Hammond parked the unmarked sedan illegally in the alley by the jail and the courts. He and Riley hopped out. Since there were no handles on the inside of the back doors, Riley quickly opened one, and Sandi slid out of the potential oven.

"I'm sure he'll be easy on you, Sandi," Riley said as they walked toward the building. "He'll want Casey for this, if what you say is true. You didn't do the murder and the fraud was coerced. He may very well let you go with no charge."

Hammond glanced at his partner but kept walking.

Sandi's nervousness had reached such a proportion that she appeared physically ill. Instead of an attractive, petite blonde, she looked like a shrunken old woman, kind of like Thelma Hardin had looked before she died.

I've got to do this, she kept telling herself. *I can't go to jail.*

Julia arrived at the courthouse and parked in the multi-level public parking where Jack and Echols had parked. She walked to the entrance and went through security the same as everyone else. Then she went upstairs to the third level, where she knew court was held. Angel was not in the hallway, but a trooper she recognized stood, leaning on the wall, too anxious to sit.

"Hi," Julia said. "Have you seen Angel?"

"Yeah, hi, Julia. He's inside. I'm up next. He should be out any minute."

"Oh, good. I have to give him his cell phone. He left it at the apartment."

"You keep him on a short leash, don't you?" the trooper laughed. "I can give it to him for you if you don't want to wait."

"Well..." Julia always felt funny receiving favors.

"You can trust me," the trooper said with mock seriousness. "I'm a cop."

Julia laughed. "Thank you," she said and handed him the phone. "And please tell him he can't get away that easily."

She turned to leave and saw Jack closing the door to a court room he had just peered into.

♠

The two detectives displayed their ID's, passed through, and waited for Sandi. Then the three of them proceeded upstairs to the escalator and began their ride up. They were half way up when Race and his entourage entered from the walkway between the courts and the jail. They entered below the escalator and out of sight of Sandi and the detectives.

Hammond arrived at the top of the moving stairs, followed closely by Riley and Sandi. As he stepped to the side and waited, he was surprised to see Jack Casey peering into one of the courtrooms.

Riley was saying, "Over here, Sandi to your..." when he noticed his partner staring, and then Casey. Both detectives glared.

"W-What is it?" Sandi asked, and then she, too, saw Jack. "Don't let him see me!" she cried, and Jack looked in their direction.

"Casey," Hammond called. "Maybe we should talk."

Jack let go of the court room door and looked toward the voice. Jack walked toward the small group, blind to Julia, who watched from down the hall. He looked from Hammond to Riley to Sandi. When his eyes got to Sandi, he glared.

"What lies have you been telling?" he fixed her with his gaze.

Riley stepped between them. "Why don't you step over here?"

"Yeah, why don't I," Jack answered, but his angry look never left Sandi's face. She couldn't meet his eyes.

Down the hallway to the right, where the judges' chambers were located, William Echols gently closed the late Judge Deaber's office door. He glanced left and right, checking to see if anyone noticed him. He looked as guilty as he was, but no one seemed interested. There were a lot of guilty looking people in the building, and most of them were guilty of one crime or another.

Echols moved nervously down the hallway toward the escalator when he spotted Jack. He quickly averted his eyes and tried to slump behind a pillar, but a woman, a Latina blocked his way. Jack saw Echols, but not Julia. She had moved behind the pillar to avoid being run into by the disheveled attorney.

"Hey! Echols!" Jack shouted.

"We have something more important to do than chat with your friends, Casey," Riley threatened, and for the second time he stepped between Jack and another person.

"Maybe we do and maybe we don't," Jack fired back. He remained calm, but his ire rose.

Echols stood in the middle of the group at the top of the escalator, looking about as inconspicuous as a penguin on a desert island.

"E-Excuse me," he stuttered, trying to get past Hammond and Sandi.

Sandi looked flustered, but she couldn't move. Hammond just glared at him. The situation deteriorated further, as, at that moment, Race and three deputies arrived at the top of the stairs.

"Excuse us, please. Prisoner, comin' through," the lead officer said, forcefully but not blatantly. He couldn't see any sense in irritating a violent man like John Racine Hardin.

Race's eyes explored the group at the top of the escalator as he arrived. His eyes grew at the sight of each face. Here were three of the people he hated most in the world, and the men who had arrested him were with them. Poisonous ecstasy roiled within him.

He grabbed the pistol that hung strapped in the holster on the officer's belt in front of him, and tugged back and to the side. The pistol restraint held for a few seconds and the officer spun past Race and into his fellow custodians. The holster fastener gave and the three jailers tumbled down the two-story escalator leaving splotches of blood and hair on the sharp, metal edges of the stairs.

Race stood at the top, close enough to touch Sandi or Hammond or Echols. Riley still had his back turned, and stood in front of Jack.

"Who wants to go first?" Race asked gleefully. He pointed the pistol at each person, one at a time, holding their undivided attention long enough for them to know who was in charge.

"How about you?"

He stiff-armed the pistol and the end of the barrel touched Sandi's head. Sandi leaned back into Hammond pinning him against a column with his arm movement restricted, so that he couldn't get to his weapon, at least not fast enough to do any good. Sandi whimpered, and for the second time in a week, fear caused her to lose control of her bladder.

Riley turned slowly as he got the gist of what was happening.

"Not again. Oh no, not again," Jack chanted, and suddenly he exploded past Riley, sending him sprawling to the tile floor.

He knocked Echols over and left the ground before he hit Race in the chest with his shoulder. Race's pistol arm went up as he fell back, and a bullet ricocheted through the three-story lobby. A woman screamed somewhere below and people hid or ran for the exit as Jack and Race tumbled down the up-escalator only to arrive at the top again. The pistol rattled up behind them. Race managed to get his shackled arms and legs between him and Jack, and, with a mighty heave, he sent Jack over the railing of the 36-foot high moving stairway.

"Jack!" Julia screamed and tried to run toward the escalator, but two strong arms grabbed her from behind. It was Angel, who had finished in court in almost the moment she had turned to leave.

Race's fallen pistol rode the stairs back up and was thumping against his head. He grabbed it before Hammond could push Sandi aside and get to his own weapon. Riley, on his feet now, yanked his 9mm pistol from the holster beneath his left arm.

"Drop it!" he shouted at Race.

"No," Race said quietly, as he calmly pointed the pistol in his hand at John Hammond. "No, I don't think I will."

"You can't get out of here," Riley countered.

"Why would I want to leave? Everyone I want to see is right here." Then, looking at Hammond, he said, "Push her over here."

"Don't shoot!" Riley shouted at the law enforcement officers below them. Several weapons were trained on Race, but no one could be certain of hitting him, and only him. Nor could they be certain that he wouldn't get a shot off even after he was hit.

"No," Hammond taunted Race with his own words. "No, I don't think I will."

Race's speed was astonishing as he clubbed the big man aside and swung his shackled arms over the cowering Sandi's head. Her arms were pinned to her sides as Race pulled her to him, pistol still in hand.

"You smell like fear," he said. "Is that how my mother smelled before you killed her?"

Jack hung by his fingers from the side of the escalator. He moved, very slowly, one hand at a time, to a point low enough to be out of danger of injuring himself in a fall. His feet touched the information counter, and the officers below thought he would climb down. They were shocked when Jack pulled himself up and quietly threw his leg over the banister. Then he gently set both feet down on a passing stair step and turned to face Race, who stood above him. Race's back was to Jack as he held Sandi hostage.

Jack remained calm. All thoughts of failure, injury or death had lost their hold on him. He was going to put an end to this once and for all.

Chapter 35

Race caught the movement in Hammond's eyes and sluggishly turned, slowed by the panicked woman in his arms. He saw Jack just before he reached the top of the stairs.

"Stop right there!" he ordered.

"Can't," Jack answered. "Escalator."

Echols, who was just getting up, dropped to the floor again.

Race squeezed off the second shot since the ordeal had begun, but Sandi encumbered his aim as she shook and sobbed. The bullet went through the right side of Jack's shirt and left a burning sensation and then a slowly growing patch of red. It shattered a huge piece of glass in the upper portion of the building, sending shards of broken glass to the ground below.

Jack never flinched; he had had enough. He arrived at the top within a split second of the gunshot and punched Sandi in the mouth, hard. Being left handed, Jack's uppercut took everyone by surprise. Sandi's head jerked to her left, followed by her body and then Race's hands. He found himself pointing the pistol at a wall in an empty corridor, and he couldn't swing Sandi's stunned, almost comatose, frame around fast enough to stop Jack's advance.

Jack let fly another left, this time a jab that caught Race on the cheekbone below his right eye. Race staggered under the force of the blow and the weight of Sandi. He let her go, but the chains on his wrists still entangled him with her. They stumbled to the ground as Race pulled the trigger over and over again, hitting wall, floor and ceiling.

Angel and Julia hid behind the column in the hallway as near misses struck around them.

Jack kept coming and went down on his right knee. He grabbed Race's gun hand and leaned on it, keeping the weapon pointed at the wall. He looked at Race and made sure Race was looking back. Then he delivered the knockout punch. Race's head hit the tile hard and came back up, but his eyes rolled back in his head and his body went limp.

Echols rose up on his knees but no higher.

Jack reached for the pistol hanging from Race's finger and Riley shouted, "Don't touch it, Casey " His weapon was leveled at Jack.

Jack paused and looked at Riley. "You've got to be kidding."

"Don't move."

Hammond had a bloody cut on the side of his forehead but seemed okay. He stepped to where Jack knelt beside the two KO's and reached over and removed the pistol from Race's hand.

He stood and backed away, and Riley said, "You're under arrest, Casey. Get up slowly and put your hands behind your back."

"You've got to be kidding," Jack repeated, and suddenly there was movement on the floor.

Race pulled Sandi tight against himself again and rolled into Jack, knocking him off balance. Jack fell to the floor as Race rose to his knees, dragging Sandi out from between his legs. He roughly moved his hands up to her neck, bruising her breasts with the chains he wore.

"Stay down, mailman," Race said in a hate-filled voice. "Stay down or I'll kill your bitch, not that you seem to care. But then I'll kill you, too."

"I should let you do it," Jack said. "She's about to tell these guys I killed your mother. I never shot anyone in my life. I'm not like you."

Race gritted his teeth with the force of holding Sandi up. She was conscious, and her hands grappled at the chains across her throat. Her face was red and croaking sounds escaped from her in fits and starts. Her legs kicked ineffectively, like a marionette.

"Oh, were you, you little bitch? I know you did it. You did it months ago. You're just using this idiot. I'll kill you and him, him for being stupid."

"Let her go, Hardin," Riley said, changing targets again. "Casey is too close. You can't strangle her before he stops you."

"I thought I was under arrest," Jack said, ignoring the gasping, red-faced woman in front of him.

"I think my partner has changed his mind," Hammond said.

Like Riley, he now had a weapon trained on Race Hardin. His arms extended over Jack's head where Jack sat on the floor.

"I'll snap her neck!" Race threatened.

"Then I'll put your lights out," Jack countered.

He rose nimbly from the floor and Hammond took a step sideways to keep a clear shot open.

Echols remained on his knees, a picture of penitent prayer.

"And what about you, hotshot attorney?" Race asked.

He looked at Echols, who looked flustered.

"I was o-on my way to see you," he stammered. "Here," he said as he flapped a piece of paper toward Race. "You can get out on bail."

"I don't think so," Riley replied without taking his eyes off Race.

"Where's the money, you ugly sonofabitch?" Race asked still looking at Echols.

He let Sandi breath in intervals, just enough to maintain her value as a living hostage.

"I'll hunt you down, you know? No place is safe. I'll find you."

"No! No, no. We can get it today. Here's the ticket."

Echols fumbled in his pocket for his wallet. Jack's eyes got big, and he almost smiled. Echols began searching every pocket and slot in the overstuffed, leather billfold. He looked determinably at first, and then the search became frantic.

"I-it's right here, I know it is."

"You bastard!" Race hollered.

Race raised his hands over Sandi's head and shoved her at Riley. Riley lowered his weapon and caught the gasping woman just as his partner squeezed the trigger of the pistol he had taken from Race.

Jack heard the click behind his head and to the left. Hammond was out of ammunition. Race was on Echols and beating him, using his chains as bludgeons. Jack jumped Race for what he hoped would be the last time. He rolled with Race into Sandi's feet and she squealed as she continued whimpering. Echols crawled like an upside down crab, an amazing feat for a man so physically out of shape.

Jack and Race rolled back toward the escalator, and Race, face down on the bottom, pushed himself and Jack to their feet. Jack spun him around and bounced him off the wall. He caught him by the shirt as he came back and redirected his momentum, just enough to send him headlong down the down-escalator.

Race lay at the bottom in a heap, blood matting his scalp where the sharp metal steps had cut him.

"Jack!" Julia called and broke free from her brother's grip.

Chapter 36

At the sound of Julia's voice, Jack jerked his gaze away from Echols. He stood as she ran toward him. Riley didn't know what to do, a rarity, and looked toward Hammond. Hammond's face, almost without movement or expression, relayed his thoughts: *It's okay. Let it go.*

Julia ran into Jack's arms, gently but firmly. He held her and smelled her hair and felt her body against his. No one spoke.

Echols whimpering and bleeding on the floor finally ruined the moment. Angel, who had been running, walked the last few feet to where the group stood. He looked down to where deputy sheriffs and EMT's were alternately trying to treat Race or injure him further. He would remain in custody this time.

Hammond looked at Echols, then yelled down the escalator, "Need some medical attention up here."

Riley sidled up to Hammond and spoke under his breath: "Remind me why we're not arresting Casey."

Intuition told him they shouldn't, but he couldn't quite piece it all together.

Hammond looked at him. "You missed that, didn't you?"

"What d'ya mean?"

"Hardin accused Casey of killing his mother, and Casey told Hardin he never shot anybody. Thelma Hardin was strangled. Sandi did it, presumably for the Social Security check. Hardin pretty much handed it to her. He wanted his mother taken care of, but he didn't want to do it himself. He never wanted to see her again."

"Oh, yeah. You're right," Riley said as a light went on in his head. "And she got taken care of, didn't she?"

Riley stepped over to the vixen who had deceived him and said, "Sandi Anderson, you're under arrest for the murder of Thelma Hardin."

She blubbered as he continued reciting her Miranda rights.

Julia loosened her grip on Jack who turned his head toward John Hammond.

"Am I under arrest, too, or have we gotten over that?"

"I think I'll let you go for now," Hammond said.

Jack turned back to Julia. "And have you gotten over thinking I'm with her?" he said, nodding in Sandi's direction.

"I thought maybe you two broke up when you punched her," Julia said. She never took her eyes off his.

"Good," he said.

Race's neck had been broken, as well as his left arm. He had a concussion and woke up in pain in a hospital bed. There were four deputy sheriffs watching the door. Their boss had threatened them: "If he gets away, you take his place."

Sandi awaited arraignment in a holding cell. She would have killed herself, but she couldn't think of how to do it.

Hammond and Riley invited Echols, who had been patched up, and Jack to an office near the jail. Julia followed Jack and Angel followed Julia.

"You're Hardin's attorney, is that right?" Riley began the questioning.

"Yes, but..." Echols just hung his head.

"It's legal to be someone's attorney, Mr., uh..."

"Echols. It's Echols."

"Okay, Mr. Echols. First, you can go back and talk to the judge if you want, but I don't think bail is gonna fly. Things have changed."

"I know. That's okay. I mean, he won't ever get out, will he?" Echols looked and acted like fear personified.

"I don't think so," Riley answered.

Then Echols told them all about how Race had contacted him. He neglected to mention the lottery ticket, hoping he would find it, cash in and separate himself from Race Hardin, Fairfax County and maybe even the US. He had to get away.

"So, Casey; I suppose you really are an innocent bystander?" Riley hated to say it.

"I suppose so," Jack replied. There was no venom, no anger and no sarcasm. Just relief.

"Okay. We'll take your word for it. So we know what happened to Thelma Hardin, who did it, and why. We know Race killed a motel clerk just to cover his tracks on the way back to even the score with Sandi. I don't know if he was angrier about her keeping the social security check or killing his mother.

"But what we don't know is why Hardin killed the two guys he worked with. Does anybody here have a clue?"

Riley didn't expect an answer and everyone looked at everyone else until Jack spoke.

"Talk to the guy at the 7-11 by Maple."

All eyes returned to Jack.

"You're starting to become my favorite suspect, again," Riley offered, breaking the silence in the room. "Why don't you enlighten us. Why we should do that?"

"Show him pictures," Jack said. "I think those guys won the lottery. I think Hardin killed them for the money."

Hammond and Riley looked at each other, eyebrows raised.

"I see the clerk there pretty often," Jack continued. "We talk. The guy said he sold the winning lottery ticket, and he thought they bought it. Especially when they quit coming around. Then we saw their pictures in the paper, at least we saw the two dead ones."

And I have the ticket, Jack thought, *and the guy at the 7-11 knows it.*

"Yeah, we'll talk to him. So, where's the ticket now?" Riley looked at Hammond.

Echols whimpered.

Jack looked at them.

Chapter 37

"Do you have any old copies of the newspaper?" Jack asked.

He and Julia were walking to the parking garage. They could see Echols up ahead, muttering and still looking through his wallet. Twice he stopped to pick up trash and then, after inspecting it, he threw it back on the ground.

"I don't, Jack," Julia said. She held his arm with both hands as if to be sure he remained among the living. Jack didn't mind, and he leaned toward her.

"Then I need to go to the library."

"Do you mind if I come?" Julia asked. "I feel like I almost lost a friend several times. I want to be with you today."

Her honesty and innocence touched Jack. He hadn't felt this way since he quit drinking, or maybe even ever.

"And why do you need to go to the library? Someone trys to kill you and you need old newspapers?" She looked up at Jack as they walked.

"C'mon. I'll tell you on the way."

At the library they found the article Jack wanted on line.

"'George Reiss,' it says, lived here in Fairfax, 'survived by wife, Ellen...' and they had kids, must be grown. We'll start with finding Ellen. George appears to be a little more...I don't know. Solid? Steady? Anyway, this other guy, Edward, could pass for a homeless person. Reminds me of me before. We'll start with George's family."

"I still can't believe this," Julia said. "And I am very proud of you."

They left the library and headed for the address given for George Reiss, deceased.

Hammond and Riley walked out of the 7-11. Actually, Hammond walked out. Riley exploded out into the heat.

"Casey is still involved in this shit I don't believe it I'm gonna kill him."

Hammond looked over the roof of the unmarked cruiser at his partner.

"We'll get to the bottom of this," Hammond replied.

He opened the door from outside the car, leaning in to turn the key. He had the AC blasting before they got in.

"Go to his house. I want him now. I want some kind of explanation. I want to kill him, or at least beat on him and arrest him!"

Hammond unleashed a rare smile. Riley didn't see it. He looked out the window through the steam coming off his face.

Jack and Julia spent the day together, drinking coke, wandering through bookstores, and finally walking around Burke Lake.

Hammond and Riley tired quickly of waiting for Jack. They left a message on his phone: "Call me right now " Riley said, and left his cell-phone number.

Echols spent the rest of the day trying to retrace every move he had made since he last saw the ticket. Hope and greed spring eternal.

♠

"You saw the sign out sheet," Hammond said. "Hardin had a lottery ticket, and Echols signed for his personal effects. Now that he's fired, he has to give them back."

"Yeah, but he didn't give back a lottery ticket. Says he must have lost it, but he's lying. He almost wet himself when I asked."

"The lottery commission will call if anyone tries to cash in. We'll get Echols or Casey or both for theft, interfering with an investigation, and anything else we can think of."

"I still want to hear what Casey has to say," Riley vented.

"I told you, I don't have it." Jack remained calm. He had driven in to see Hammond and Riley, because he didn't want them at his house anymore.

"You're lying You and Echols are up to something," Riley menaced.

"Check with the lottery commission. Probably the rightful owner will turn it in."

Silence. Riley looked at Hammond, then back at Casey.

"The rightful own*ers*," Riley emphasized, "are dead. The ticket belongs to Hardin, who doesn't deserve it. He doesn't even deserve his next breath. It should go to...." He paused.

Riley's eyes bored into Jack, angry at first, and then a slow grin began to spread over his Irish mug. He turned red with embarrassment, but also with a kind of jealous admiration.

"You didn't. Are you saying you never had the ticket?"

"Never."

"How would you have gotten it if you had had it?" Riley almost laughed.

Jack hesitated, then said, "If I gave an attorney a ride home after he wrecked his car, and he gave me a couple of bucks with a lottery ticket in between them, I guess that would be part of my tip. Then I would have had it."

"And you wouldn't have kept 11 million bucks?" Riley asked.

"Nah. You would have caught me cashing it in...That is, if I ever had it."

A week later Jack sorted mail, getting ready to deliver his route for the first time since his suspension. He had a large amount of mail that should have been forwarded but hadn't been. Some had nasty notes written across them, things like, "Hasn't lived here in 15 years!" and "CAN'T YOU READ!" He also had a few hold orders but no mail to go with them, so he would be bringing that back at the end of the day. Another pile of mail had bad addresses, and the subs didn't recognise the names. Fortunately, Jack did.

Morey remained Morey. No extra time to clean up the mess, no help. Jack would surely be late getting out of the office and even later getting back; probably get a reprimand.

Ah, but is it worth it, he thought.

Julia walked up behind him, a pleasant, unexpected interruption. Someone had to collect the tubs of undeliverable bulk rate mail everyday. Today Julia helped the distribution clerks. She had finished sorting the PO Box mail.

"So nice of you to come back to work, Jack," she said.

They had been together often, almost daily, since the fiasco with Sandi, Hardin and the rest.

"Oh, thank-you," he mocked. "And how are you today? Do you love it here?"

"Oh, jes. It's becoming funner and funner."

They both laughed.

"Get back to work, Casey," growled Morey. "You ask for overtime, and now you want to stand around? You're lucky I don't fire you."

"I'm sorry!" Julia whispered and touched his arm as she moved away. Jack winked at her.

Then he yelled at the back the retreating ugly man, "Why is so much of this mail dated last week, Morey? Did you suspend everybody?"

Hammond hung up the phone.

"Guess who won the lottery?" Before Riley could answer, he said, "Two women named Ellen and Sharyl. Imagine that."

"Gee," Riley effervesced, "imagine that."

A month later, Jack drove his reupholstered, recarpeted, repainted, rebuilt Chevrolet to Julia and Angel's apartment. Ellen and Sharyl had given him a nice tip. A finders fee, of sorts. Now he would take Julia to dinner in style.

"Take care of my sister, holmes, or I take care of you," Angel said.

"No problem, Angel. She's safe with me."

"Yeah, right! Didn't she have to save your ass in the grocery store."

"Hey, watch your language," Julia scolded as she entered the room. "And I don't want my two favourite hombres fighting with each other."

"We're not fighting," Angel said. "Look. He's still standing up."

Jack started forward saying, "Okay, okay. Now you're going down."

Julia stepped between them. Angel laughed as he used her to shield himself from the impending blows.

"Don't hit me, white boy. I've seen what you can do…"

"And don't forget it," Jack admonished.

"…when you hit a girl," Angel finished and the mock battle continued.